W9-BXB-428

CONTEMPORARY AMERICAN FICTION

GHOSTS

Paul Auster is the author of *The Invention of Solitude* as well as four books of poetry and a volume of essays, *The Art of Hunger*. In addition he has translated numerous works from the French and is the editor of *The Random House Book of Twentieth-Century French Poetry*. He has twice received literary fellowships from the National Endowment for the Arts and is the pseudonymous author of a popular detective novel. *City of Glass* (Penguin) and *The Locked Room* (soon to be published by Penguin) are the first and third volumes of *The New York Trilogy*. His latest novel, *In the Country of Last Things*, is being published by Viking.

GHOSTS

by Paul Auster

The New York Trilogy, volume 2

PENGUIN BOOKS

PENGUIN BOOKS
Viking Penguin Inc., 40 West 23rd Street,
New York, New York 10010, U.S.A.
Penguin Books Ltd, Harmondsworth,
Middlesex, England
Penguin Books Australia Ltd, Ringwood,
Victoria, Australia
Penguin Books Canada Limited, 2801 John Street,
Markham, Ontario, Canada L3R 1B4
Penguin Books (N.Z.) Ltd, 182–190 Wairau Road,
Auckland 10, New Zealand

First published in the United States of America by
Sun & Moon Press 1986
Published in Penguin Books 1987

Publication of this book was made possible, in part, through a
grant from the National Endowment for the Arts and through
contributions to the Contemporary Arts Educational Project, Inc.

LIBRARY OF CONGRESS CATALOGING IN PUBLICATION DATA
Auster, Paul, 1947–
Ghosts.
(The New York trilogy; v. 2)
I. Title. II. Series: Auster, Paul,
1947–   New York trilogy; v. 2.
PS3551.U77G46   1987   813'.54   86-22660
ISBN 0 14 00.9735 X

Printed in the United States of America by
R. R. Donnelley & Sons Company, Harrisonburg, Virginia
Set in Bodoni

Also by Paul Auster

Prose

White Spaces (1980)
The Invention of Solitude (1982)
The Art of Hunger (1982)
City of Glass (1985)
The Locked Room (1986)
In the Country of Last Things (1987)

Poetry

Unearth (1974)
Wall Writing (1976)
Fragments from Cold (1977)
Facing the Music (1980)

Editor

*The Random House Book of Twentieth Century
   French Poetry* (1982)

First of all there is Blue. Later there is White, and then there is Black, and before the beginning there is Brown. Brown broke him in, Brown taught him the ropes, and when Brown grew old, Blue took over. That is how it begins. The place is New York, the time is the present, and neither one will ever change. Blue goes to his office every day and sits at his desk, waiting for something to happen. For a long time nothing does, and then a man named White walks through the door, and that is how it begins.

The case seems simple enough. White wants Blue to follow a man named Black and to keep an eye on him for as long as necessary. While working for Brown, Blue did many tail jobs, and this one seems no different, perhaps even easier than most.

Blue needs the work, and so he listens to White and doesn't ask many questions. He assumes it's a marriage case and that White is a jealous husband. White doesn't elaborate. He wants a weekly report, he says, sent to such and such a postbox number, typed out in duplicate on pages so long and so wide. A check will be sent each week to Blue in the mail. White then tells Blue where Black lives, what he looks like, and so on. When Blue asks White how long he thinks the case will last, White says he doesn't know. Just keep sending the reports, he says, until further notice.

To be fair to Blue, he finds it all a little strange. But to say that he has misgivings at this point would be going too far. Still, it's impossible for him not to notice certain things about White. The black beard, for example, and the overly bushy eyebrows. And then there is the skin, which seems inordinately white, as though covered with powder. Blue is no amateur in the art of disguise, and it's not difficult for him to see through this one. Brown was his teacher, after all, and in his day Brown was the best in the business. So Blue begins to think he was wrong, that the case has nothing to do with marriage. But he gets no farther than this, for White is still speaking to him, and Blue must concentrate on following his words.

Everything has been arranged, White says. There's a small apartment directly across the street from Black's. I've already rented it, and you can move in there today. The rent will be paid for until the case is over.

Good idea, says Blue, taking the key from White. That will eliminate the legwork.

Exactly, White answers, stroking his beard.

And so it's settled. Blue agrees to take the job, and they shake hands on it. To show his good faith, White even gives Blue an advance of ten fifty-dollar bills.

That is how it begins, then. The young Blue and a man named White, who is obviously not the man he appears to be. It doesn't matter, Blue says to himself after White has left. I'm sure he has his reasons. And besides, it's not my problem. The only thing I have to worry about is doing my job.

It is February 3, 1947. Little does Blue know, of course, that the case will go on for years. But the present is no less dark than the past, and its mystery is equal to anything the future might hold. Such is the way of the world: one step at a time, one word and then the next. There are certain things that Blue cannot possibly know at this point. For knowledge comes slowly, and when it comes, it is often at great personal expense.

White leaves the office, and a moment later Blue picks up the phone and calls the future Mrs. Blue. I'm going under cover, he tells his sweetheart. Don't worry if I'm out of touch for a little while. I'll be thinking of you the whole time.

Blue takes a small gray satchel down from the shelf and packs it with his thirty-eight, a pair of binoculars, a notebook, and other tools of the trade. Then he tidies his desk, puts his papers in order, and locks up the office. From there he goes to the apartment that White has rented for him. The address is unimportant. But let's say Brooklyn Heights, for the sake of argument. Some quiet, rarely traveled street not far from the bridge—Orange Street perhaps. Walt Whitman handset the first edition of Leaves of Grass on this street in 1855, and it was here that Henry Ward Beecher railed against slavery from the pulpit of his red-brick church. So much for local color.

It's a small studio apartment on the third floor of a four-story brownstone. Blue is happy to see that it's fully equipped, and as he walks around the room inspecting the furnishings, he discovers that everything in the place is new: the bed, the table, the chair, the rug, the linens, the kitchen supplies, everything. There is a complete set of clothes hanging in the closet, and Blue, wondering if the clothes are meant for him, tries them on and sees that they fit. It's not the biggest place I've ever been in, he says to himself, pacing from one end of the room to the other, but it's cozy enough, cozy enough.

He goes back outside, crosses the street, and enters the opposite building. In the entryway he searches for Black's name on one of the mailboxes and finds it: Black—3rd floor. So far so good. Then he returns to his room and gets down to business.

Parting the curtains of the window, he looks out and sees Black sitting at a table in his room across the street. To the extent that Blue can make out what is happening, he gathers that Black is writing. A look through the binoculars confirms that he is. The lenses, however, are not powerful enough to pick up the writing itself, and even if they were, Blue doubts that he would be able to read the handwriting upside down. All he can say for certain, therefore, is that

Black is writing in a notebook with a red fountain pen. Blue takes out his own notebook and writes: Feb. 3, 3 P.M. Black writing at his desk.

Now and then Black pauses in his work and gazes out the window. At one point, Blue thinks that he is looking directly at him and ducks out of the way. But on closer inspection he realizes that it is merely a blank stare, signifying thought rather than seeing, a look that makes things invisible, that does not let them in. Black gets up from his chair every once in a while and disappears to a hidden spot in the room, a corner Blue supposes, or perhaps the bathroom, but he is never gone for very long, always returning promptly to the desk. This goes on for several hours, and Blue is none the wiser for his efforts. At six o'clock he writes the second sentence in his notebook: This goes on for several hours.

It's not so much that Blue is bored, but that he feels thwarted. Without being able to read what Black has written, everything is a blank so far. Perhaps he's a madman, Blue thinks, plotting to blow up the world. Perhaps that writing has something to do with his secret formula. But Blue is immediately embarrassed by such a childish notion. It's too early to know anything, he says to himself, and for the time being he decides to suspend judgment.

His mind wanders from one small thing to another, eventually settling on the future Mrs. Blue. They were planning to go out tonight, he remembers, and if it hadn't been for White showing up at the office today and this new case, he would be with her now. First the Chinese restaurant on 39th Street, where they would have wrestled with the chopsticks and held hands under the table, and then the double feature at the Paramount. For a brief moment he has a startlingly clear picture of her face in his mind (laughing with lowered eyes, feigning embarrassment), and he realizes that he would much rather be with her than sitting in this little room for God knows how long. He thinks about calling her up on the phone for a chat, hesitates, and then decides against it. He doesn't want to seem weak. If she knew how much he needed her, he would begin to lose his advantage, and that wouldn't be good. The man must always be the stronger one.

Black has now cleared his table and replaced the writing materials with dinner. He sits there chewing slowly, staring out the window in that abstracted way of his. At the sight of food, Blue realizes that he is hungry and hunts through the kitchen cabinet for something to eat. He settles on a meal of canned stew and soaks up the gravy with a slice of white bread. After dinner he has some hope that Black will be going outside, and he is encouraged when he sees a sudden flurry of activity in Black's room. But all comes to nothing. Fifteen minutes later, Black is sitting at his desk again, this time reading a book. A lamp is on beside him, and Blue has a clearer view of Black's face than before. Blue estimates Black's age to be the same as his, give or take a year or two.

That is to say, somewhere in his late twenties or early thirties. He finds Black's face pleasant enough, with nothing to distinguish it from a thousand other faces one sees every day. This is a disappointment to Blue, for he is still secretly hoping to discover that Black is a madman. Blue looks through the binoculars and reads the title of the book that Black is reading. Walden, by Henry David Thoreau. Blue has never heard of it before and writes it down carefully in his notebook.

So it goes for the rest of the evening, with Black reading and Blue watching him read. As time passes, Blue grows more and more discouraged. He's not used to sitting around like this, and with the darkness closing in on him now, it's beginning to get on his nerves. He likes to be up and about, moving from one place to another, doing things. I'm not the Sherlock Holmes type, he would say to Brown, whenever the boss gave him a particularly sedentary task. Give me something I can sink my teeth into. Now, when he himself is the boss, this is what he gets: a case with nothing to do. For to watch someone read and write is in effect to do nothing. The only way for Blue to have a sense of what is happening is to be inside Black's mind, to see what he is thinking, and that of course is impossible. Little by little, therefore, Blue lets his own mind drift back to the old days. He thinks of Brown and some of the cases they worked on together, savoring the memory of their triumphs. There was the Redman Affair, for example, in which they tracked down the bank teller who had embezzled a quarter of a million dollars. For that one Blue pretended to be a bookie and lured Redman into placing a bet with him. The money was traced back to the bills missing from the bank, and the man got what was coming to him. Even better was the Gray Case. Gray had been missing for over a year, and his wife was ready to give him up for dead. Blue searched through all the normal channels and came up empty. Then, one day, as he was about to file his final report, he stumbled on Gray in a bar, not two blocks from where the wife was sitting, convinced he would never return. Gray's name was now Green, but Blue knew it was Gray in spite of this, for he had been carrying around a photograph of the man for the past three months and knew his face by heart. It turned out to be amnesia. Blue took Gray back to his wife, and although he didn't remember her and continued to call himself Green, he found her to his liking and some days later proposed marriage. So Mrs. Gray became Mrs. Green, married to the same man a second time, and while Gray never remembered the past—and stubbornly refused to admit that he had forgotten anything—that did not seem to stop him from living comfortably in the present. Whereas Gray had worked as an engineer in his former life, as Green he now kept the job as bartender in the bar two blocks away. He liked mixing the drinks, he said, and talking to the people who came in, and he couldn't imagine doing anything else. I was born to be a bartender, he announced

to Brown and Blue at the wedding party, and who were they
to object to what a man chose to do with his life?

Those were the good old days, Blue says to himself now,
as he watches Black turn off the light in his room across the
street. Full of strange twists and amusing coincidences.
Well, not every case can be exciting. You've got to take the
good with the bad.

Blue, ever the optimist, wakes up the next morning in a
cheerful mood. Outside, snow is falling on the quiet street,
and everything has turned white. After watching Black eat
his breakfast at the table by the window and read a few
more pages of Walden, Blue sees him retreat to the back of
the room and then return to the window dressed in his
overcoat. The time is shortly after eight o'clock. Blue
reaches for his hat, his coat, his muffler, and boots, hastily
scrambles into them, and gets downstairs to the street less
than a minute after Black. It is a windless morning, so still
that he can hear the snow falling on the branches of the
trees. No one else is about, and Black's shoes have made a
perfect set of tracks on the white pavement. Blue follows the
tracks around the corner and then sees Black ambling down
the next street, as if enjoying the weather. Not the behavior
of a man about to escape, Blue thinks, and accordingly he
slows his pace. Two streets later, Black enters a small
grocery store, stays ten or twelve minutes, and then comes
out with two heavily loaded brown paper bags. Without
noticing Blue, who is standing in a doorway across the

street, he begins retracing his steps towards Orange Street. Stocking up for the storm, Blue says to himself. Blue then decides to risk losing contact with Black and goes into the store himself to do the same. Unless it's a decoy, he thinks, and Black is planning to dump the groceries and take off, it's fairly certain that he's on his way home. Blue therefore does his own shopping, stops in next door to buy a newspaper and several magazines, and then returns to his room on Orange Street. Sure enough, Black is already at his desk by the window, writing in the same notebook as the day before.

Because of the snow, visibility is poor, and Blue has trouble deciphering what is happening in Black's room. Even the binoculars don't help much. The day remains dark, and through the endlessly falling snow, Black appears to be no more than a shadow. Blue resigns himself to a long wait and then settles down with his newspapers and magazines. He is a devoted reader of True Detective and tries never to miss a month. Now, with time on his hands, he reads the new issue thoroughly, even pausing to read the little notices and ads on the back pages. Buried among the feature stories on gangbusters and secret agents, there is one short article that strikes a chord in Blue, and even after he finishes the magazine, he finds it difficult not to keep thinking about it. Twenty-five years ago, it seems, in a patch of woods outside Philadelphia, a little boy was found murdered. Although the police promptly began work on the case, they never managed to come up with any clues. Not only did they have no suspects, they could not even identify the boy. Who he was, where he had come from, why he was there—all these questions remained unanswered. Eventually, the case was dropped from the active file, and if not for the coroner who had been assigned to do the autopsy on the boy, it would have been forgotten altogether. This man, whose name was Gold, became obsessed by the murder. Before the child was buried, he made a death mask of his face, and from then on devoted whatever time he could to the mystery. After twenty years, he reached retirement age, left his job, and began spending every moment on the case. But things did not go well. He made no headway, came not one step closer to solving the crime. The article in True Detective describes how he is now offering a reward of two thousand dollars to anyone who can provide information about the little boy. It also includes a grainy, retouched photograph of the man holding the death mask in his hands. The look in his eyes is so haunted and imploring that Blue can scarcely turn his own eyes away. Gold is growing old now, and he is afraid that he will die before he solves the case. Blue is deeply moved by this. If it were possible, he would like nothing better than to drop what he's doing and try to help Gold. There aren't enough men like that, he thinks. If the boy were Gold's son, then it would make sense: revenge, pure and simple, and anyone can understand that. But the boy was a complete stranger to him, and so there's nothing personal about it, no hint of a secret motive. It is this thought that so affects Blue. Gold refuses to accept a world in which the murderer of a child can go unpunished, even if the murderer himself is now dead, and he is willing to sacrifice his own life and happiness to right the wrong. Blue then thinks about the little boy for a while, trying to imagine what really happened, trying to feel what the boy must have felt, and then it dawns on him that the murderer must have been one of the parents, for otherwise the boy would have been reported as missing. That only makes it worse, Blue thinks, and as he begins to grow sick at the thought of it, fully understanding now what Gold must feel all the time, he realizes that twenty-five years ago he too was a little boy and that had the boy lived he would be Blue's age now. It could have been me, Blue thinks. I could have been that little boy. Not knowing what else to do, he cuts out the picture from the magazine and tacks it onto the wall above his bed.

So it goes for the first days. Blue watches Black, and little of anything happens. Black writes, reads, eats, takes brief strolls through the neighborhood, seems not to notice that Blue is there. As for Blue, he tries not to worry. He assumes that Black is lying low, biding his time until the right moment comes. Since Blue is only one man, he realizes that constant vigilance is not expected of him. After all, you can't watch someone twenty-four hours a day. There has to be time for you to sleep, to eat, to do your laundry, and so on. If White wanted Black to be watched around the clock, he would have hired two or three men, not one. But Blue is only one, and more than what is possible he cannot do.

Still, he does begin to worry, in spite of what he tells himself. For if Black must be watched, then it would follow that he must be watched every hour of every day. Anything less than constant surveillance would be as no surveillance at all. It would not take much, Blue reasons, for the entire picture to change. A single moment's inattention—a glance to the side of him, a pause to scratch his head, the merest yawn—and presto, Black slips away and commits whatever heinous act he is planning to commit. And yet, there will necessarily be such moments, hundreds and even thousands of them every day. Blue finds this troubling, for no matter how often he turns this problem over inside himself, he gets no closer to solving it. But that is not the only thing that troubles him.

Until now, Blue has not had much chance for sitting still, and this new idleness has left him at something of a loss. For the first time in his life, he finds that he has been thrown back on himself, with nothing to grab hold of, nothing to distinguish one moment from the next. He has never given much thought to the world inside him, and though he always knew it was there, it has remained an unknown quantity, unexplored and therefore dark, even to himself. He has moved rapidly along the surface of things for as long as he can remember, fixing his attention on these surfaces only in order to perceive them, sizing up one and then passing on to the next, and he has always taken pleasure in the world as such, asking no more of things than that they be there. And until now they have been, etched vividly against the daylight, distinctly telling him what they are, so perfectly themselves and nothing else that he has never had to pause before them or look twice. Now, suddenly, with the world as it were removed from him, with nothing much to see but a vague shadow by the name of Black, he finds himself thinking about things that have never occurred to him before, and this, too, has begun to trouble him. If thinking is perhaps too strong a word at this point, a slightly more modest term—speculation, for example— would not be far from the mark. To speculate, from the Latin speculatus, meaning to spy out, to observe, and linked to the word speculum, meaning mirror or looking glass. For in spying out at Black across the street, it is as though Blue were looking into a mirror, and instead of merely watching another, he finds that he is also watching himself. Life has slowed down so drastically for him that Blue is now able to see things that have previously escaped his attention. The trajectory of the light that passes through the room each day, for example, and the way the sun at certain hours will reflect the snow on the far corner of the ceiling in his room. The beating of his heart, the sound of his breath, the blinking of his eyes—Blue is now aware of these tiny events, and try as he might to ignore them, they persist in his mind like a nonsensical phrase repeated over and over again. He knows it cannot be true, and yet little by little this phrase seems to be taking on a meaning.

Of Black, of White, of the job he has been hired to do, Blue now begins to advance certain theories. More than just helping to pass the time, he discovers that making up stories can be a pleasure in itself. He thinks that perhaps White and Black are brothers and that a large sum of money is at stake—an inheritance, for example, or the capital invested in a partnership. Perhaps White wants to prove that Black is incompetent, have him committed to an institution, and take control of the family fortune himself. But Black is too clever for that and has gone into hiding, waiting for the pressure to ease up. Another theory that Blue puts forward has White and Black as rivals, both of them racing toward the same goal—the solution to a scientific problem, for example—and White wants Black watched in order to be sure he isn't outsmarted. Still another story has it that White is a renegade agent from the F.B.I. or some espionage organization, perhaps foreign, and has struck out on his own to conduct some peripheral investigation not necessarily sanctioned by his superiors. By hiring Blue to do his work for him, he can keep the surveillance of Black a secret and at the same time continue to perform his normal duties. Day by day, the list of these stories grows, with Blue sometimes returning in his mind to an early story to add certain flourishes and details and at other times starting over again with something new. Murder plots, for instance, and kidnapping schemes for giant ransoms. As the days go on, Blue realizes there is no end to the stories he can tell. For Black is no more than a kind of blankness, a hole in the texture of things, and one story can fill this hole as well as any other.

Blue does not mince words, however. He knows that more than anything else he would like to learn the real story. But at this early stage he also knows that patience is called for. Bit by bit, therefore, he begins to dig in, and with each day that passes he finds himself a little more comfortable with his situation, a little more resigned to the fact that he is in for the long haul.

Unfortunately, thoughts of the future Mrs. Blue occasionally disturb his growing peace of mind. Blue misses her more than ever, but he also senses somehow that things will never be the same again. Where this feeling comes from he cannot tell. But while he feels reasonably content whenever he confines his thoughts to Black, to his room, to the case he is working on, whenever the future Mrs. Blue enters his consciousness, he is seized by a kind of panic. All of a sudden, his calm turns to anguish, and he feels as though he is falling into some dark, cave-like place, with no hope of finding a way out. Nearly every day he has been tempted to pick up the phone and call her, thinking that perhaps a moment of real contact would break the spell. But the days pass, and still he doesn't call. This, too, is troubling to him,

for he cannot remember a time in his life when he has been
so reluctant to do a thing he so clearly wants to do. I'm
changing, he says to himself. Little by little, I'm no longer
the same. This interpretation reassures him somewhat, at
least for a while, but in the end it only leaves him feeling
stranger than before. The days pass, and it becomes
difficult for him not to keep seeing pictures of the future
Mrs. Blue in his head, especially at night, and there in the
darkness of his room, lying on his back with his eyes open,
he reconstructs her body piece by piece, beginning with her
feet and ankles, working his way up her legs and along her
thighs, climbing from her belly toward her breasts, and
then, roaming happily among the softness, dipping down to
her buttocks and then up again along her back, at last
finding her neck and curling forward to her round and
smiling face. What is she doing now? he sometimes asks
himself. And what does she think of all this? But he can
never come up with a satisfactory answer. If he is able to
invent a multitude of stories to fit the facts concerning
Black, with the future Mrs. Blue all is silence, confusion,
and emptiness.

The day comes for him to write his first report. Blue is an
old hand at such compositions and has never had any
trouble with them. His method is to stick to outward facts,
describing events as though each word tallied exactly with
the thing described, and to question the matter no further.
Words are transparent for him, great windows that stand

between him and the world, and until now they have never impeded his view, have never even seemed to be there. Oh, there are moments when the glass gets a trifle smudged and Blue has to polish it in one spot or another, but once he finds the right word, everything clears up. Drawing on the entries he has made previously in his notebook, sifting through them to refresh his memory and to underscore pertinent remarks, he tries to fashion a coherent whole, discarding the slack and embellishing the gist. In every report he has written so far, action holds forth over interpretation. For example: The subject walked from Columbus Circle to Carnegie Hall. No references to the weather, no mention of the traffic, no stab at trying to guess what the subject might be thinking. The report confines itself to known and verifiable facts, and beyond this limit it does not try to go.

Faced with the facts of the Black case, however, Blue grows aware of his predicament. There is the notebook, of course, but when he looks through it to see what he has written, he is disappointed to find such paucity of detail. It's as though his words, instead of drawing out the facts and making them sit palpably in the world, have induced them to disappear. This has never happened to Blue before. He looks out across the street and sees Black sitting at his desk as usual. Black, too, is looking through the window at that moment, and it suddenly occurs to Blue that he can no longer depend on the old procedures. Clues, legwork, investigative routine—none of this is going to matter any-more. But then, when he tries to imagine what will replace these things, he gets nowhere. At this point, Blue can only surmise what the case is not. To say what it is, however, is completely beyond him.

Blue sets his typewriter on the table and casts about for ideas, trying to apply himself to the task at hand. He thinks that perhaps a truthful account of the past week would include the various stories he has made up for himself concerning Black. With so little else to report, these excursions into the make-believe would at least give some flavor of what has happened. But Blue brings himself up short, realizing that they have nothing really to do with Black. This isn't the story of my life, after all, he says. I'm supposed to be writing about him, not myself.

Still, it looms as a perverse temptation, and Blue must struggle with himself for some time before fighting it off. He goes back to the beginning and works his way through the case, step by step. Determined to do exactly what has been asked of him, he painstakingly composes the report in the old style, tackling each detail with such care and aggravat-ing precision that many hours go by before he manages to finish. As he reads over the results, he is forced to admit that everything seems accurate. But then why does he feel so dissatisfied, so troubled by what he has written? He says to himself: what happened is not really what happened. For the first time in his experience of writing reports, he discovers that words do not necessarily work, that it is possible for them to obscure the things they are trying to say. Blue looks around the room and fixes his attention on various objects, one after the other. He sees the lamp and says to himself, lamp. He sees the bed and says to himself, bed. He sees the notebook and says to himself, notebook. It will not do to call the lamp a bed, he thinks, or the bed a lamp. No, these words fit snugly around the things they stand for, and the moment Blue speaks them, he feels a deep satisfaction, as though he has just proved the existence of the world. Then he looks out across the street and sees Black's window. It is dark now, and Black is asleep. That's the problem, Blue says to himself, trying to find a little courage. That and nothing else. He's there, but it's impossible to see him. And even when I do see him it's as though the lights are out.

He seals up his report in an envelope and goes outside, walks to the corner, and drops it into the mailbox. I may not be the smartest person in the world, he says to himself, but I'm doing my best, I'm doing my best.

After that, the snow begins to melt. The next morning, the sun is shining brightly, clusters of sparrows are chirping in the trees, and Blue can hear the pleasant dripping of water from the edge of the roof, the branches, the lampposts. Spring suddenly does not seem far away. Another few weeks, he says to himself, and every morning will be like this one.

Black takes advantage of the weather to wander farther afield than previously, and Blue follows. Blue is relieved to be moving again, and as Black continues on his way, Blue hopes the journey will not end before he's had a chance to work out the kinks. As one would imagine, he has always been an ardent walker, and to feel his legs striding along through the morning air fills him with happiness. As they move through the narrow streets of Brooklyn Heights, Blue is encouraged to see that Black keeps increasing his distance from home. But then, his mood suddenly darkens. Black begins to climb the staircase that leads to the walkway across the Brooklyn Bridge, and Blue gets it into his head that he's planning to jump. Such things happen, he tells himself. A man goes to the top of the bridge, gives a last look to the world through the wind and the clouds, and then leaps out over the water, bones cracking on impact, his body broken apart. Blue gags on the image, tells himself to stay alert. If anything starts to happen, he decides, he will step out from his role as neutral bystander and intervene. For he does not want Black to be dead—at least not yet.

It has been many years since Blue crossed the Brooklyn Bridge on foot. The last time was with his father when he was a boy, and the memory of that day comes back to him now. He can see himself holding his father's hand and walking at his side, and as he hears the traffic moving along the steel bridge-road below, he can remember telling his father that the noise sounded like the buzzing of an enormous swarm of bees. To his left is the Statue of Liberty; to his right is Manhattan, the buildings so tall in the morning sun they seem to be figments. His father was a great one for facts, and he told Blue the stories of all the monuments and skyscrapers, vast litanies of detail—the architects, the dates, the political intrigues—and how at one time the Brooklyn Bridge was the tallest structure in America. The old man was born the same year the bridge was finished, and there was always that link in Blue's mind, as though the bridge were somehow a monument to his father. He liked the story he was told that day as he and Blue Senior walked home over the same wooden planks he was walking on now, and for some reason he never forgot it. How John Roebling, the designer of the bridge, got his foot crushed between the dock pilings and a ferry boat just days after finishing the plans and died from gangrene in less than three weeks. He didn't have to die, Blue's father said, but the only treatment he would accept was hydrotherapy, and that proved useless, and Blue was struck that a man who had spent his life building bridges over bodies of water so that people wouldn't get wet should believe that the only true medicine consisted in immersing oneself in water. After John Roebling's death, his son Washington took over as chief engineer, and that was another curious story. Washington Roebling was just thirty-one at the time, with no building experience except for the wooden bridges he designed during the Civil War, but he proved to be even more brilliant than his father. Not long after construction began on the Brooklyn Bridge, however, he was trapped for several hours during a fire in one of the underwater caissons and came out of it with a severe case of the bends, an excruciating disease in which nitrogen bubbles gather in the bloodstream. Nearly killed by the attack, he was thereafter an invalid, unable to leave the top floor room where he and his wife set up house in Brooklyn Heights. There Washington Roebling sat every day for many years, watching the progress of the bridge through a telescope, sending his wife down every morning with his instructions, drawing elaborate color pictures for the foreign workers who spoke no English so they would understand what to do next, and the remarkable thing was that the whole bridge was literally in his head: every piece of it had been memorized, down to the tiniest bits of steel and stone, and though Washington Roebling never set foot on the bridge, it was totally present inside him, as though by the end of all those years it had somehow grown into his body.

Blue thinks of this now as he makes his way across the river, watching Black ahead of him and remembering his father and his boyhood out in Gravesend. The old man was a cop, later a detective at the 77th precinct, and life would have been good, Blue thinks, if it hadn't been for the Russo Case and the bullet that went through his father's brain in 1927. Twenty years ago, he says to himself, suddenly appalled by the time that has passed, wondering if there is a heaven, and if so whether or not he will get to see his father again after he dies. He remembers a story from one of the endless magazines he has read this week, a new monthly called Stranger than Fiction, and it seems somehow to follow from all the other thoughts that have just come to him. Somewhere in the French Alps, he recalls, a man was lost skiing twenty or twenty-five years ago, swallowed up by an avalanche, and his body was never recovered. His son, who was a little boy at the time, grew up and also became a skier. One day in the past year he went skiing, not far from the spot where his father was lost— although he did not know this. Through the minute and persistent displacements of the ice over the decades since his father's death, the terrain was now completely different from what it had been. All alone there in the mountains, miles away from any other human being, the son chanced upon a body in the ice—a dead body, perfectly intact, as though preserved in suspended animation. Needless to say, the young man stopped to examine it, and as he bent down and looked at the face of the corpse, he had the distinct and terrifying impression that he was looking at himself. Trembling with fear, as the article put it, he inspected the body more closely, all sealed away as it was in the ice, like someone on the other side of a thick window, and saw that it was his father. The dead man was still young, even younger than his son was now, and there was something awesome about it, Blue felt, something so odd and terrible about being older than your own father, that he actually had to fight back tears as he read the article. Now, as he nears the end of the bridge, these same feelings come back to him, and he wishes to God that his father could be there, walking over the river and telling him stories. Then, suddenly aware of what his mind is doing, he wonders why he has turned so sentimental, why all these thoughts keep coming to him, when for so many years they have never even occurred to him. It's all part of it, he thinks, embarrassed at himself for being like this. That's what happens when you have no one to talk to.

He comes to the end and sees that he was wrong about Black. There will be no suicides today, no jumping from bridges, no leaps into the unknown. For there goes his man, as blithe and unperturbed as anyone can be, descending the stairs of the walkway and traveling along the street that curves around City Hall, then moving north along Centre Street past the courthouse and other municipal buildings, never once slackening his pace, continuing on through Chinatown and beyond. These divagations last several hours, and at no point does Blue have the sense that Black is walking to any purpose. He seems rather to be airing his lungs, walking for the pure pleasure of walking, and as the journey goes on Blue confesses to himself for the first time that he is developing a certain fondness for Black.

At one point Black enters a bookstore and Blue follows him in. There Black browses for half an hour or so, accumulating a small pile of books in the process, and Blue, with nothing better to do, browses as well, all the while trying to keep his face hidden from Black. The little glances he takes when Black seems not to be looking give him the feeling that he has seen Black before, but he can't remember where. There's something about the eyes, he says to himself, but that's as far as he gets, not wanting to call attention to himself and not really sure if there's anything to it.

A minute later, Blue comes across a copy of Walden by Henry David Thoreau. Flipping through the pages, he is surprised to discover that the name of the publisher is Black: "Published for the Classics Club by Walter J. Black, Inc., Copyright 1942." Blue is momentarily jarred by this coincidence, thinking that perhaps there is some message in it for him, some glimpse of meaning that could make a difference. But then, recovering from the jolt, he begins to think not. It's a common enough name, he says to himself— and besides, he knows for a fact that Black's name is not Walter. Could be a relative though, he adds, or maybe even his father. Still turning this last point over in his mind, Blue decides to buy the book. If he can't read what Black writes, at least he can read what he reads. A long shot, he says to himself, but who knows that it won't give some hint of what the man is up to.

So far so good. Black pays for his books, Blue pays for his book, and the walk continues. Blue keeps looking for some pattern to emerge, for some clue to drop in his path

that will lead him to Black's secret. But Blue is too honest
a man to delude himself, and he knows that no rhyme or
reason can be read into anything that's happened so far.
For once, he is not discouraged by this. In fact, as he
probes more deeply into himself, he realizes that on the
whole he feels rather invigorated by it. There is something
nice about being in the dark, he discovers, something
thrilling about not knowing what is going to happen next. It
keeps you alert, he thinks, and there's no harm in that, is
there? Wide awake and on your toes, taking it all in, ready
for anything.

A few moments after thinking this thought, Blue is finally
offered a new development, and the case takes on its first
twist. Black turns a corner in midtown, walks halfway down
the block, hesitates briefly, as if searching for an address,
backtracks a few paces, moves on again, and several
seconds later enters a restaurant. Blue follows him in,
thinking nothing much of it, since it's lunchtime after all,
and people have to eat, but it does not escape him that
Black's hesitation seems to indicate that he's never been
here before, which in turn might mean that Black has an
appointment. It's a dark place inside, fairly crowded, with
a group of people clustered around the bar in front, lots of
chatter and the clinking of silverware and plates in the
background. It looks expensive, Blue thinks, with wood
paneling on the walls and white tablecloths, and he decides
to keep his bill as low as he can. Tables are available, and

Blue takes it as a good omen when he is seated within eyeshot of Black, not obtrusively close, but not so far as not to be able to watch what he does. Black tips his hand by asking for two menus, and three or four minutes later breaks into a smile when a woman walks across the room, approaches Black's table, and kisses him on the cheek before sitting down. The woman's not bad, Blue thinks. A bit on the lean side for his taste, but not bad at all. Then he thinks: now the interesting part begins.

Unfortunately, the woman's back is turned to Blue, so he can't watch her face as the meal progresses. As he sits there eating his Salisbury steak, he thinks that maybe his first hunch was the right one, that it's a marriage case after all. Blue is already imagining the kinds of things he will write in his next report, and it gives him pleasure to contemplate the phrases he will use to describe what he is seeing now. By having another person in the case, he knows that certain decisions have to be made. For example: should he stick with Black or divert his attention to the woman? This could possibly accelerate matters a bit, but at the same time it could mean that Black would be given the chance to slip away from him, perhaps for good. In other words, is the meeting with the woman a smoke-screen or the real thing? Is it a part of the case or not, is it an essential or contingent fact? Blue ponders these questions for a while and concludes that it's too early to tell. Yes, it could be one thing, he tells himself. But it could also be another.

About midway through the meal, things seem to take a turn for the worse. Blue detects a look of great sadness in Black's face, and before he knows it the woman seems to be crying. At least that is what he can gather from the sudden change in the position of her body: her shoulders slumped, her head leaning forward, her face perhaps covered by her hands, the slight shuddering along her back. It could be a fit of laughter, Blue reasons, but then why would Black be so miserable? It looks as though the ground has just been cut out from under him. A moment later, the woman turns her face away from Black, and Blue gets a glimpse of her in profile: tears without question, he thinks, as he watches her dab her eyes with a napkin and sees a smudge of wet mascara glistening on her cheek. She stands up abruptly and walks off in the direction of the ladies' room. Again Blue has an unobstructed view of Black, and seeing that sadness in his face, that look of absolute dejection, he almost begins to feel sorry for him. Black glances in Blue's direction, but clearly he's not seeing anything, and then, an instant later, he buries his face in his hands. Blue tries to guess what is happening, but it's impossible to know. It looks like it's over between them, he thinks, it has the feeling of something that's come to an end. And yet, for all that, it could just be a tiff.

The woman returns to the table looking a little better, and then the two of them sit there for a few minutes without saying anything, leaving their food untouched. Black sighs

once or twice, looking off into the distance, and finally calls
for the check. Blue does the same and then follows the two
of them out of the restaurant. He notes that Black has his
hand on her elbow, but that could just be a reflex he tells
himself, and probably means nothing. They walk down the
street in silence, and at the corner Black waves down a cab.
He opens the door for the woman, and before she climbs in
he touches her very gently on the cheek. She gives him a
brave little smile in return, but still they don't say a word.
Then she sits down in the back seat, Black shuts the door,
and the cab takes off.

Black walks around for a few minutes, pausing briefly in
front of a travel agency window to study a poster of the
White Mountains, and then climbs into a cab himself. Blue
gets lucky again and manages to find another cab just
seconds later. He tells the driver to follow Black's cab and
then sits back as the two yellow cars make their way slowly
through the traffic downtown, across the Brooklyn Bridge,
and finally to Orange Street. Blue is shocked by the fare
and kicks himself mentally for not following the woman
instead. He should have known that Black was going home.

His mood brightens considerably when he enters his
building and finds a letter in his mailbox. It can only be one
thing, he tells himself, and sure enough, as he walks
upstairs and opens the envelope, there it is: the first check,
a postal money order for the exact amount settled on with
White. He finds it a bit perplexing, however, that the

method of payment should be so anonymous. Why not a personal check from White? This leads Blue to toy with the thought that White is a renegade agent after all, eager to cover his tracks and therefore making sure there will be no record of the payments. Then, removing his hat and overcoat and stretching out on the bed, Blue realizes that he's a little disappointed not to have had some comment about the report. Considering how hard he struggled to get it right, a word of encouragement would have been welcomed. The fact that the money was sent means that White was not dissatisfied. But still silence is not a rewarding response, no matter what it means. If that's the way it is, Blue says to himself, I'll just have to get used to it.

The days go by, and once again things settle down to the barest of routines. Black writes, reads, shops in the neighborhood, visits the post office, takes an occasional stroll. The woman does not reappear, and Black makes no further excursions to Manhattan. Blue begins to think that any day he will get a letter telling him the case is closed. The woman is gone, he reasons, and that could be the end of it. But nothing of the sort happens. Blue's meticulous description of the scene in the restaurant draws no special response from White, and week after week the checks continue to arrive on time. So much for love, Blue says to himself. The woman never meant anything. She was just a diversion.

In this early period, Blue's state of mind can best be described as one of ambivalence and conflict. There are moments when he feels so completely in harmony with Black, so naturally at one with the other man, that to anticipate what Black is going to do, to know when he will stay in his room and when he will go out, he need merely look into himself. Whole days go by when he doesn't even bother to look through the window or follow Black onto the street. Now and then, he even allows himself to make solo expeditions, knowing full well that during the time he is gone Black will not have budged from his spot. How he knows this remains something of a mystery to him, but the fact is that he is never wrong, and when the feeling comes over him, he is beyond all doubt and hesitation. On the other hand, not all moments are like these. There are times when he feels totally removed from Black, cut off from him in a way that is so stark and absolute that he begins to lose the sense of who he is. Loneliness envelops him, shuts him in, and with it comes a terror worse than anything he has ever known. It puzzles him that he should switch so rapidly from one state to another, and for a long time he goes back and forth between extremes, not knowing which one is true and which one false.

After a stretch of particularly bad days, he begins to long for some companionship. He sits down and writes a detailed letter to Brown, outlining the case and asking for his advice. Brown has retired to Florida, where he spends most of his time fishing, and Blue knows that it will take quite a while before he receives an answer. Still, the day after he mails the letter, he begins looking forward to the reply with an eagerness that soon grows to obsession. Each morning, about an hour before the mail is delivered, he plants himself by the window, watching for the postman to round the corner and come into view, pinning all his hopes on what Brown will say to him. What he is expecting from this letter is not certain. Blue does not even ask the question, but surely it is something monumental, some luminous and extraordinary words that will bring him back to the world of the living.

As the days and weeks go by without any letter from Brown, Blue's disappointment grows into an aching, irrational desperation. But that is nothing compared to what he feels when the letter finally comes. For Brown does not even address himself to what Blue wrote. It's good to hear from you, the letter begins, and good to know you're working so hard. Sounds like an interesting case. Can't say I miss any of it, though. Here it's the good life for me—get up early and fish, spend some time with the wife, read a little, sleep in the sun, nothing to complain about. The only thing I don't understand is why I didn't move down here years ago.

The letter goes on in that vein for several pages, never once broaching the subject of Blue's torments and anxieties. Blue feels betrayed by the man who was once like a father to him, and when he finishes the letter he feels empty, the stuffing all knocked out of him. I'm on my own, he thinks, there's no one to turn to anymore. This is followed by several hours of despondency and self-pity, with Blue thinking once or twice that maybe he'd be better off dead. But eventually he works his way out of the gloom. For Blue is a solid character on the whole, less given to dark thoughts than most, and if there are moments when he feels the world is a foul place, who are we to blame him for it? By the time supper rolls around, he has even begun to look on the bright side. This is perhaps his greatest talent: not that he does not despair, but that he never despairs for very long. It might be a good thing after all, he says to himself. It might be better to stand alone than to depend on anyone else. Blue thinks about this for a while and decides there is something to be said for it. He is no longer an apprentice. There is no master above him anymore. I'm my own man, he says to himself. I'm my own man, accountable to no one but myself.

Inspired by this new approach to things, he discovers that he has at last found the courage to contact the future Mrs. Blue. But when he picks up the phone and dials her number, there is no answer. This is a disappointment, but he remains undaunted. I'll try again some other time, he says. Some time soon.

The days continue to pass. Once again, Blue falls into step with Black, perhaps even more harmoniously than before. In doing so, he discovers the inherent paradox of his situation. For the closer he feels to Black, the less he finds it necessary to think about him. In other words, the

more deeply entangled he becomes, the freer he is. What
bogs him down is not involvement but separation. For it is
only when Black seems to drift away from him that he must
go out looking for him, and this takes time and effort, not
to speak of struggle. At those moments when he feels closest
to Black, however, he can even begin to lead the semblance
of an independent life. At first he is not very daring in what
he allows himself to do, but even so he considers it a kind
of triumph, almost an act of bravery. Going outside, for
example, and walking up and down the block. Small as it
might be, this gesture fills him with happiness, and as he
moves back and forth along Orange Street in the lovely
spring weather, he is glad to be alive in a way he has not felt
in years. At one end there is a view of the river, the harbor,
the Manhattan skyline, the bridges. Blue finds all this
beautiful, and on some days he even allows himself to sit for
several minutes on one of the benches and look out at the
boats. In the other direction there is the church, and
sometimes Blue goes to the small grassy yard to sit for a
while, studying the bronze statue of Henry Ward Beecher.
Two slaves are holding on to Beecher's legs, as though
begging him to help them, to make them free at last, and in
the brick wall behind there is a porcelain relief of Abraham
Lincoln. Blue cannot help but feel inspired by these images,
and each time he comes to the churchyard his head fills with
noble thoughts about the dignity of man.

Little by little, he becomes more bold in his strayings

from Black. It is 1947, the year that Jackie Robinson breaks in with the Dodgers, and Blue follows his progress closely, remembering the churchyard and knowing there is more to it than just baseball. One bright Tuesday afternoon in May, he decides to make an excursion to Ebbetts Field, and as he leaves Black behind in his room on Orange Street, hunched over his desk as usual with his pen and papers, he feels no cause for worry, secure in the fact that everything will be exactly the same when he returns. He rides the subway, rubs shoulders with the crowd, feels himself lunging towards a sense of the moment. As he takes his seat at the ball park, he is struck by the sharp clarity of the colors around him: the green grass, the brown dirt, the white ball, the blue sky above. Each thing is distinct from every other thing, wholly separate and defined, and the geometric simplicity of the pattern impresses Blue with its force. Watching the game, he finds it difficult to take his eyes off Robinson, lured constantly by the blackness of the man's face, and he thinks it must take courage to do what he is doing, to be alone like that in front of so many strangers, with half of them no doubt wishing him to be dead. As the game moves along, Blue finds himself cheering whatever Robinson does, and when the black man steals a base in the third inning he rises to his feet, and later, in the seventh, when Robinson doubles off the wall in left, he actually pounds the back of the man next to him for joy. The Dodgers pull it out in the ninth with a sacrifice fly, and

as Blue shuffles off with the rest of the crowd and makes his
way home, it occurs to him that Black did not cross his
mind even once.

But ball games are only the beginning. On certain nights,
when it is clear to Blue that Black will not be going
anywhere, he slips out to a bar not far away for a beer or
two, enjoying the conversations he sometimes has with the
bartender, whose name is Red, and who bears an uncanny
resemblance to Green, the bartender from the Gray Case so
long ago. A blowsy tart named Violet is often there, and
once or twice Blue gets her tipsy enough to get invited back
to her place around the corner. He knows that she likes him
well enough because she never makes him pay for it, but he
also knows that it has nothing to do with love. She calls him
honey and her flesh is soft and ample, but whenever she has
one drink too many she begins to cry, and then Blue has to
console her, and he secretly wonders if it's worth the
trouble. His guilt towards the future Mrs. Blue is scant,
however, for he justifies these sessions with Violet by
comparing himself to a soldier at war in another country.
Every man needs a little comfort, especially when his
number could be up tomorrow. And besides, he isn't made
of stone, he says to himself.

More often than not, however, Blue will bypass the bar
and go to the movie theater several blocks away. With
summer coming on now and the heat beginning to hover
uncomfortably in his little room, it's refreshing to be able to

sit in the cool theater and watch the feature show. Blue is
fond of the movies, not only for the stories they tell and the
beautiful women he can see in them, but for the darkness of
the theater itself, the way the pictures on the screen are
somehow like the thoughts inside his head whenever he
closes his eyes. He is more or less indifferent to the kinds of
movies he sees, whether comedies or dramas, for example,
or whether the film is shot in black and white or in color,
but he has a particular weakness for movies about detec-
tives, since there is a natural connection, and he is always
gripped by these stories more than by others. During this
period he sees a number of such movies and enjoys them all:
Lady in the Lake, Fallen Angel, Dark Passage, Body and
Soul, Ride the Pink Horse, Desperate, and so on. But for
Blue there is one that stands out from the rest, and he likes
it so much that he actually goes back the next night to see
it again.

It's called Out of the Past, and it stars Robert Mitchum
as an ex-private eye who is trying to build a new life for
himself in a small town under an assumed name. He has a
girl friend, a sweet country girl named Ann, and runs a gas
station with the help of a deaf-and-dumb boy, Jimmy, who
is firmly devoted to him. But the past catches up with
Mitchum, and there's little he can do about it. Years ago, he
had been hired to look for Jane Greer, the mistress of
gangster Kirk Douglas, but once he found her they fell in
love and ran off together to live in secret. One thing led to

another—money was stolen, a murder was committed—and eventually Mitchum came to his senses and left Greer, finally understanding the depth of her corruption. Now he is being blackmailed by Douglas and Greer into committing a crime, which itself is merely a set-up, for once he figures out what is happening, he sees that they are planning to frame him for another murder. A complicated story unfolds, with Mitchum desperately trying to extricate himself from the trap. At one point, he returns to the small town where he lives, tells Ann that he's innocent, and again persuades her of his love. But it's really too late, and Mitchum knows it. Towards the end, he manages to convince Douglas to turn in Greer for the murder she committed, but at that moment Greer enters the room, calmly takes out a gun, and kills Douglas. She tells Mitchum that they belong to each other, and he, fatalistic to the last, appears to go along. They decide to escape the country together, but as Greer goes to pack her bag, Mitchum picks up the phone and calls the police. They get into the car and drive off, but soon they come to a police roadblock. Greer, seeing that she's been double-crossed, pulls a gun from her bag and shoots Mitchum. The police then open fire on the car and Greer is killed as well. After that, there's one last scene—the next morning, back in the small town of Bridgeport. Jimmy is sitting on a bench outside the gas station, and Ann walks over and sits down beside him. Tell me one thing, Jimmy, she says, I've got to know this one thing: was he running away with her or not? The boy thinks for a moment, trying to decide between truth and kindness. Is it more important to preserve his friend's good name or to spare the girl? All this happens in no more than an instant. Looking into the girl's eyes, he nods his head, as if to say yes, he was in love with Greer after all. Ann pats Jimmy's arm and thanks him, then walks off to her former boyfriend, a straight-arrow local policeman who always despised Mitchum. Jimmy looks up at the gas station sign with Mitchum's name on it, gives a little salute of friendship, and then turns away and walks down the road. He is the only one who knows the truth, and he will never tell.

For the next few days, Blue goes over this story many times in his head. It's a good thing, he decides, that the movie ends with the deaf mute boy. The secret is buried, and Mitchum will remain an outsider, even in death. His ambition was simple enough: to become a normal citizen in a normal American town, to marry the girl next door, to live a quiet life. It's strange, Blue thinks, that the new name Mitchum chooses for himself is Jeff Bailey. This is remarkably close to the name of another character in a movie he saw the previous year with the future Mrs. Blue—George Bailey, played by James Stewart in It's a Wonderful Life. That story was also about small town America, but from the opposite point of view: the frustrations of a man who spends his whole life trying to escape. But in the end he comes to understand that his life has been a good one, that he has done the right thing all along. Mitchum's Bailey would no doubt like to be the same man as Stewart's Bailey. But in his case the name is false, a product of wishful thinking. His real name is Markham—or, as Blue sounds it out to himself, mark him—and that is the whole point. He has been marked by the past, and once that happens, nothing can be done about it. Something happens, Blue thinks, and then it goes on happening forever. It can never be changed, can never be otherwise. Blue begins to be haunted by this thought, for he sees it as a kind of warning, a message delivered up from within himself, and try as he does to push it away, the darkness of this thought does not leave him.

One night, therefore, Blue finally turns to his copy of Walden. The time has come, he says to himself, and if he doesn't make an effort now, he knows that he never will. But the book is not a simple business. As Blue begins to read, he feels as though he is entering an alien world. Trudging through swamps and brambles, hoisting himself up gloomy screes and treacherous cliffs, he feels like a prisoner on a forced march, and his only thought is to escape. He is bored by Thoreau's words and finds it difficult to concentrate. Whole chapters go by, and when he comes to the end of them he realizes that he has not retained a thing. Why would anyone want to go off and live alone in the woods? What's all this about planting beans and not drinking coffee or eating meat? Why all these interminable descriptions of birds? Blue thought that he was going to get a story, or at least something like a story, but this is no more than blather, an endless harangue about nothing at all.

It would be unfair to blame him, however. Blue has never read much of anything except newspapers and magazines, and an occasional adventure novel when he was a boy. Even experienced and sophisticated readers have been known to have trouble with Walden, and no less a figure than Emerson once wrote in his journal that reading Thoreau made him feel nervous and wretched. To Blue's credit, he does not give up. The next day he begins again, and this second go-through is somewhat less rocky than the first. In the third chapter he comes across a sentence that finally says something to him—Books must be read as deliberately and reservedly as they were written—and suddenly he understands that the trick is to go slowly, more slowly than he has ever gone with words before. This helps to some extent, and certain passages begin to grow clear: the business about clothes in the beginning, the battle between the red ants and the black ants, the argument against work. But Blue still finds it painful, and though he grudgingly admits that Thoreau is perhaps not as stupid as he thought, he begins to resent Black for putting him through this torture. What he does not know is that were he to find the patience to read the book in the spirit in which it asks to be read, his entire life would begin to change, and little by little he would come to a full understanding of his situation—that is to say, of Black, of White, of the case, of everything that concerns him. But lost chances are as much a part of life as chances taken, and a story cannot dwell on what might have been. Throwing the book aside in disgust, Blue puts on his coat (for it is fall now) and goes out for a breath of air. Little does he realize that this is the beginning of the end. For something is about to happen, and once it happens, nothing will ever be the same again.

He goes to Manhattan, wandering farther from Black than at any time before, venting his frustration in movement, hoping to calm himself down by exhausting his body. He walks north, alone in his thoughts, not bothering to take in the things around him. On East 26th Street his left shoelace comes undone, and it is precisely then, as he bends down to tie it, crouching on one knee, that the sky falls on top of him. For who should he glimpse at just that moment but the future Mrs. Blue. She is coming up the street with her two arms linked through the right arm of a man Blue has never seen before, and she is smiling radiantly, engrossed in what the man is saying to her. For several moments Blue is so at a loss that he doesn't know whether to bend his head farther down and hide his face or stand up and greet the woman whom he now understands—with a knowledge as sudden and irrevocable as the slamming of a door—will never be his wife. As it turns out, he manages neither—first ducking his head, but then discovering a second later that he wants her to recognize him, and when he sees she will not, being so wrapped up in her companion's talk, Blue abruptly rises from the pavement when they are no more than six feet away from him. It is as though some spectre has suddenly materialized in front of her, and the ex-future Mrs. Blue gives out a little gasp, even before she sees who the spectre is. Blue speaks her name, in a voice that seems strange to him, and she stops dead in her tracks. Her face registers the shock of seeing Blue—and then, rapidly, her expression turns to one of anger.

You! she says to him. You!

Before he has a chance to say a word, she disentangles herself from her companion's arm and begins pounding Blue's chest with her fists, screaming insanely at him, accusing him of one foul crime after another. It is all Blue can do to repeat her name over and over, as though trying desperately to distinguish between the woman he loves and the wild beast who is now attacking him. He feels totally defenseless, and as the onslaught continues, he begins to welcome each new blow as just punishment for his behavior. The other man soon puts a stop to it, however, and though Blue is tempted to take a swing at him, he is too stunned to act quickly enough, and before he knows it the man has led away the weeping ex-future Mrs. Blue down the street and around the corner, and that's the end of it.

This brief scene, so unexpected and devastating, turns Blue inside out. By the time he regains his composure and manages to return home, he realizes that he has thrown away his life. It's not her fault, he says to himself, wanting to blame her but knowing he can't. He might have been dead for all she knew, and how can he hold it against her for wanting to live? Blue feels tears forming in his eyes, but more than grief he feels anger at himself for being such a fool. He has lost whatever chance he might have had for happiness, and if that is the case, then it would not be wrong to say that this is truly the beginning of the end.

Blue gets back to his room on Orange Street, lies down on his bed, and tries to weigh the possibilities. Eventually, he turns his face to the wall and encounters the photograph of the coroner from Philadelphia, Gold. He thinks of the sad blankness of the unsolved case, the child lying in his grave with no name, and as he studies the death mask of the little boy, he begins to turn an idea over in his mind. Perhaps there are ways of getting close to Black, he thinks, ways that need not give him away. God knows there must be. Moves that can be made, plans that can be set in motion—perhaps two or three at the same time. Never mind the rest, he tells himself. It's time to turn the page.

His next report is due the day after tomorrow, and so he sits down to it now in order to get it mailed off on schedule. For the past few months his reports have been exceedingly cryptic, no more than a paragraph or two, giving the bare bones and nothing else, and this time he does not depart from the pattern. However, at the bottom of the page he interjects an obscure comment as a kind of test, hoping to elicit something more than silence from White: Black seems ill. I'm afraid he might be dying. Then he seals up the report, saying to himself that this is only the beginning.

Two days hence, Blue hastens early in the morning to the Brooklyn Post Office, a great castle of a building within eyeshot of the Manhattan Bridge. All of Blue's reports have been addressed to box number one thousand and one, and he walks over to it now as though by accident, sauntering past it and unobtrusively peeking inside to see if the report has come. It has. Or at least a letter is there—a solitary white envelope tilted at a forty-five degree angle in the narrow cubby—and Blue has no reason to suspect it's any letter other than his own. He then begins a slow circular walk around the area, determined to remain until White or someone working for White appears, his eyes fixed on the huge wall of numbered boxes, each box with a different combination, each one holding a different secret. People come and go, open boxes and close them, and Blue keeps wandering in his circle, pausing every now and then in some random spot and then moving on. Everything seems brown to him, as though the fall weather outside has penetrated the room, and the place smells pleasantly of cigar smoke. After several hours he begins to get hungry, but he does not give in to the call of his stomach, telling himself it's now or never and therefore holding his ground. Blue watches everyone who approaches the bank of post boxes, zeroing in on each person who skirts the vicinity of one thousand and one, aware of the fact that if it's not White who comes for the reports it could be anyone—an old woman, a young child, and consequently he must take nothing for granted. But none of these possibilities comes to anything, for the box remains untouched throughout, and though Blue momentarily and successively spins a story for each candidate who comes near, trying to imagine how that person might be connected to White and or Black, what role he or she might play in the case, and so on, one by one he is forced to dismiss them from his mind, casting them back into the oblivion from which they have come.

Just past noon, at a moment when the post office begins to get crowded—an influx of people on their lunch break rushing through to mail letters, buy stamps, attend to business of one sort or another—a man with a mask on his face walks through the door. Blue doesn't notice him at first, what with so many others coming through the door at the same time, but as the man separates himself from the crowd and begins walking toward the numbered post boxes, Blue finally catches sight of the mask—a mask of the sort that children wear on Halloween, made of rubber and portraying some hideous monster with gashes in his forehead and bleeding eyeballs and fangs for teeth. The rest of him is perfectly ordinary (gray tweed overcoat, red scarf wrapped around his neck), and Blue senses in this first moment that the man behind the mask is White. As the man continues walking toward the area of box one thousand and one, this sense grows to conviction. At the same time, Blue also feels that the man is not really there, that even though he knows he is seeing him, it is more than likely that he is the only one who can. On this point, however, Blue is wrong, for as the masked man continues moving across the vast marble floor, Blue sees a number of people laughing and pointing at him—but whether this is better or worse he cannot say. The masked man reaches box one thousand and one, spins the combination wheel back and forth and back again, and opens the box. As soon as Blue sees that this is definitely his man, he begins making a move toward him, not really sure of what he is planning to do, but in the back of his mind no doubt intending to grab hold of him and tear the mask off his face. But the man is too alert, and once he has pocketed the envelope and locked the box, he gives a quick glance around the room, sees Blue approaching, and makes a dash for it, heading for the door as fast as he can. Blue runs after him, hoping to catch him from behind and tackle him, but he gets tangled momentarily in a crowd of people at the door, and by the time he manages to get through it, the masked man is bounding down the stairs, landing on the sidewalk, and running down the street. Blue continues in pursuit, even feels he is gaining ground, but then the man reaches the corner, where a bus just happens to be pulling out from a stop, and so he conveniently leaps aboard, and Blue is left in the lurch, all out of breath and standing there like an idiot.

Two days later, when Blue receives his check in the mail,

there is finally a word from White. No more funny business, it says, and though it's not much of a word, for all that Blue is glad to have received it, happy to have cracked White's wall of silence at last. It's not clear to him, however, whether the message refers to the last report or to the incident in the post office. After thinking it over for a while, he decides that it makes no difference. One way or another, the key to the case is action. He must go on disrupting things wherever he can, a little here, a little there, chipping away at each conundrum until the whole structure begins to weaken, until one day the whole rotten business comes toppling to the ground.

Over the next few weeks, Blue returns to the post office several times, hoping to catch another glimpse of White. But nothing comes of it. Either the report is already gone from the box when he gets there, or White does not show up. The fact that this area of the post office is open twenty-four hours a day leaves Blue with few options. White is on to him now, and he will not make the same mistake twice. He will simply wait until Blue is gone before going to the box, and unless Blue is willing to spend his entire life in the post office, there's no way he can expect to sneak up on White again.

The picture is far more complicated than Blue ever imagined. For almost a year now, he has thought of himself as essentially free. For better or worse he has been doing his job, looking straight ahead of him and studying Black, waiting for a possible opening, trying to stick with it, but through it all he has not given a single thought to what might be going on behind him. Now, after the incident with the masked man and the further obstacles that have ensued, Blue no longer knows what to think. It seems perfectly plausible to him that he is also being watched, observed by another in the same way that he has been observing Black. If that is the case, then he has never been free. From the very start he has been the man in the middle, thwarted in front and hemmed in on the rear. Oddly enough, this thought reminds him of some sentences from Walden, and he searches through his notebook for the exact phrasing, fairly certain that he has written them down. We are not where we are, he finds, but in a false position. Through an infirmity of our natures, we suppose a case, and put ourselves into it, and hence are in two cases at the same time, and it is doubly difficult to get out. This makes sense to Blue, and though he is beginning to feel a little frightened, he thinks that perhaps it is not too late for him to do something about it.

The real problem boils down to identifying the nature of the problem itself. To start with, who poses the greater threat to him, White or Black? White has kept up his end of the bargain: the checks have come on time every week, and to turn against him now, Blue knows, would be to bite the hand that feeds him. And yet White is the one who set the case in motion—thrusting Blue into an empty room, as it were, and then turning off the light and locking the door. Ever since, Blue has been groping about in the darkness, feeling blindly for the light switch, a prisoner of the case itself. All well and good, but why would White do such a thing? When Blue comes up against this question, he can no longer think. His brain stops working, he can get no farther than this.

Take Black, then. Until now he has been the entire case, the apparent cause of all his troubles. But if White is really out to get Blue and not Black, then perhaps Black has nothing to do with it, perhaps he is no more than an innocent bystander. In that case, it is Black who occupies the position Blue has assumed all along to be his, and Blue who takes the role of Black. There is something to be said for this. On the other hand, it is also possible that Black is somehow working in league with White and that together they have conspired to do Blue in.

If so, what are they doing to him? Nothing very terrible, finally—at least not in any absolute sense. They have trapped Blue into doing nothing, into being so inactive as to reduce his life to almost no life at all. Yes, says Blue to himself, that's what it feels like: like nothing at all. He feels like a man who has been condemned to sit in a room and go on reading a book for the rest of his life. This is strange enough—to be only half alive at best, seeing the world only through words, living only through the lives of others. But if the book were an interesting one, perhaps it wouldn't be so bad. He could get caught up in the story, so to speak, and little by little begin to forget himself. But this book offers him nothing. There is no story, no plot, no action—nothing but a man sitting alone in a room and writing a book. That's all there is, Blue realizes, and he no longer wants any part of it. But how to get out? How to get out of the room that is the book that will go on being written for as long as he stays in the room?

As for Black, the so-called writer of this book, Blue can no longer trust what he sees. Is it possible that there really is such a man—who does nothing, who merely sits in his room and writes? Blue has followed him everywhere, has tracked him down into the remotest corners, has watched him so hard that his eyes seem to be failing him. Even when he does leave his room, Black never goes anywhere, never does much of anything: grocery shopping, an occasional haircut, a trip to the movies, and so on. But mostly he just wanders around the streets, looking at odd bits of scenery, clusters of random data, and even this happens only in spurts. For a while it will be buildings—craning his neck to catch a glimpse of the roofs, inspecting doorways, running his hands slowly over the stone facades. And then, for a week or two, it will be public statues, or the boats in the river, or the signs in the street. Nothing more than that, with scarcely a word to anyone, and no meetings with others except for that one lunch with the woman in tears by now so long ago. In one sense, Blue knows everything there is to know about Black: what kind of soap he buys, what newspapers he reads, what clothes he wears, and each of these things he has faithfully recorded in his notebook. He has learned a thousand facts, but the only thing they have taught him is that he knows nothing. For the fact remains that none of this is possible. It is not possible for such a man as Black to exist.

Consequently, Blue begins to suspect that Black is no more than a ruse, another one of White's hirelings, paid by the week to sit in that room and do nothing. Perhaps all that writing is merely a sham—page after page of it: a list of every name in the phone book, for example, or each word from the dictionary in alphabetical order, or a handwritten copy of Walden. Or perhaps they are not even words, but senseless scribbles, random marks of a pen, a growing heap of nonsense and confusion. This would make White the real writer then—and Black no more than his stand-in, a fake, an actor with no substance of his own. Then there are the times, following through with this thought, that Blue believes the only logical explanation is that Black is not one man but several. Two, three, four look-alikes who play the role of Black for Blue's benefit, each one putting in his allotted time and then going back to the comforts of hearth and home. But this is a thought too monstrous for Blue to contemplate for very long. Months go by, and at last he says to himself out loud: I can't breathe anymore. This is the end. I'm dying.

It is midsummer, 1948. Finally mustering the courage to

act, Blue reaches into his bag of disguises and casts about for a new identity. After dismissing several possibilities, he settles on an old man who used to beg on the corners of his neighborhood when he was a boy—a local character by the name of Jimmy Rose—and decks himself out in the garb of tramphood: tattered woolen clothes, shoes held together with string to prevent the soles from flapping, a weathered carpetbag to hold his belongings, and then, last of all, a flowing white beard and long white hair. These final details give him the look of an Old Testament prophet. Blue as Jimmy Rose is not a scrofulous down-and-outer so much as a wise fool, a saint of penury living in the margins of society. A trifle daft perhaps, but harmless: he exudes a sweet indifference to the world around him, for since everything has happened to him already, nothing can disturb him anymore.

Blue posts himself in a suitable spot across the street, takes a fragment of a broken magnifying glass from his pocket, and begins reading a crumpled day-old newspaper that he has salvaged from one of the nearby garbage cans. Two hours later, Black appears, walking down the steps of his house and then turning in Blue's direction. Black pays no attention to the bum—either lost in his own thoughts or ignoring him on purpose—and so as he begins to approach, Blue addresses him in a pleasant voice.

Can you spare some change, mister?

Black stops, looks over the disheveled creature who has just spoken, and gradually relaxes into a smile as he realizes he is not in danger. Then he reaches into his pocket, pulls out a coin, and puts it in Blue's hand.

Here you are, he says.

God bless you, says Blue.

Thank you, answers Black, touched by the sentiment.

Never fear, says Blue. God blesses all.

And with that word of reassurance, Black tips his hat to Blue and continues on his way.

The next afternoon, once again in bum's regalia, Blue waits for Black in the same spot. Determined to keep the conversation going a little longer this time, now that he has won Black's confidence, Blue finds that the problem is taken out of his hands when Black himself shows an eagerness to linger. It is late in the day by now, not yet dusk but no longer afternoon, the twilight hour of slow changes, of glowing bricks and shadows. After greeting the bum cordially and giving him another coin, Black hesitates a moment, as though debating whether to take the plunge, and then says:

Has anyone ever told you that you look just like Walt Whitman?

Walt who? answers Blue, remembering to play his part.

Walt Whitman. A famous poet.

No, says Blue. I can't say I know him.

You wouldn't know him, says Black. He's not alive anymore. But the resemblance is remarkable.

Well, you know what they say, says Blue. Every man has his double somewhere. I don't see why mine can't be a dead man.

The funny thing, continues Black, is that Walt Whitman used to work on this street. He printed his first book right here, not far from where we're standing.

You don't say, says Blue, shaking his head pensively. It makes you stop and think, doesn't it?

There are some odd stories about Whitman, Black says, gesturing to Blue to sit down on the stoop of the building behind them, which he does, and then Black does the same, and suddenly it's just the two of them out there in the summer light together, chatting away like two old friends about this and that.

Yes, says Black, settling in comfortably to the languor of the moment, a number of very curious stories. The one about Whitman's brain, for example. All his life Whitman believed in the science of phrenology—you know, reading the bumps on the skull. It was very popular at the time.

Can't say I've ever heard of it, replies Blue.

Well, that doesn't much matter, says Black. The main thing is that Whitman was interested in brains and skulls— thought they could tell you everything about a man's character. Anyway, when Whitman lay dying over there in New Jersey about fifty or sixty years ago, he agreed to let them perform an autopsy on him after he was dead.

How could he agree to it after he was dead?

Ah, good point. I didn't say it right. He was still alive when he agreed. He just wanted them to know that he didn't mind if they opened him up later. What you might call his dying wish.

Famous last words.

That's right. A lot of people thought he was a genius, you see, and they wanted to take a look at his brain to find out if there was anything special about it. So, the day after he died, a doctor removed Whitman's brain—cut it right out of his head—and had it sent to the American Anthropometric Society to be measured and weighed.

Like a giant cauliflower, interjects Blue.

Exactly. Like a big gray vegetable. But this is where the story gets interesting. The brain arrives at the laboratory, and just as they're about to get to work on it, one of the assistants drops it on the floor.

Did it break?

Of course it broke. A brain isn't very tough, you know. It splattered all over the place, and that was that. The brain of America's greatest poet got swept up and thrown out with the garbage.

Blue, remembering to respond in character, emits several wheezing laughs—a good imitation of an old codger's mirth. Black laughs, too, and by now the atmosphere has thawed to such an extent that no one could ever know they were not lifelong chums.

It's sad to think of poor Walt lying in his grave, though, says Black. All alone and without any brains.

Just like that scarecrow, says Blue.

Sure enough, says Black. Just like the scarecrow in the land of Oz.

After another good laugh, Black says: And then there's the story of the time Thoreau came to visit Whitman. That's a good one, too.

Was he another poet?

Not exactly. But a great writer just the same. He's the one who lived alone in the woods.

Oh yes, says Blue, not wanting to carry his ignorance too far. Someone once told me about him. Very fond of nature he was. Is that the man you mean?

Precisely, answers Black. Henry David Thoreau. He came down from Massachusetts for a little while and paid a call on Whitman in Brooklyn. But the day before that he came right here to Orange Street.

Any particular reason?

Plymouth Church. He wanted to hear Henry Ward Beecher's sermon.

A lovely spot, says Blue, thinking of the pleasant hours he has spent in the grassy yard. I like to go there myself.

Many great men have gone there, says Black. Abraham Lincoln, Charles Dickens—they all walked down this street and went into the church.

Ghosts.

Yes, there are ghosts all around us.

And the story?

It's really very simple. Thoreau and Bronson Alcott, a friend of his, arrived at Whitman's house on Myrtle Avenue, and Walt's mother sent them up to the attic bedroom he shared with his mentally retarded brother, Eddy. Everything was just fine. They shook hands, exchanged greetings, and so on. But then, when they sat down to discuss their views of life, Thoreau and Alcott noticed a full chamber pot right in the middle of the floor. Walt was of course an expansive fellow and paid no attention, but the two New Englanders found it hard to keep talking with a bucket of excrement in front of them. So eventually they went downstairs to the parlor and continued the conversation there. It's a minor detail, I realize. But still, when two great writers meet, history is made, and it's important to get all the facts straight. That chamber pot, you see, somehow reminds me of the brains on the floor. And when you stop to think about it, there's a certain similarity of form. The bumps and convolutions, I mean. There's a definite connection. Brains and guts, the insides of a man. We always talk about trying to get inside a writer to understand his work better. But when you get right down to it, there's not much to find in there—at least not much that's different from what you'd find in anyone else.

You seem to know a lot about these things, says Blue, who's beginning to lose the thread of Black's argument.

It's my hobby, says Black. I like to know how writers live, especially American writers. It helps me to understand things.

I see, says Blue, who sees nothing at all, for with each word Black speaks, he finds himself understanding less and less.

Take Hawthorne, says Black. A good friend of Thoreau's, and probably the first real writer America ever had. After he graduated from college, he went back to his mother's house in Salem, shut himself up in his room, and didn't come out for twelve years.

What did he do in there?

He wrote stories.

Is that all? He just wrote?

Writing is a solitary business. It takes over your life. In some sense, a writer has no life of his own. Even when he's there, he's not really there.

Another ghost.

Exactly.

Sounds mysterious.

It is. But Hawthorne wrote great stories, you see, and we still read them now, more than a hundred years later. In one of them, a man named Wakefield decides to play a joke on his wife. He tells her that he has to go away on a business trip for a few days, but instead of leaving the city, he goes around the corner, rents a room, and just waits to see what will happen. He can't say for sure why he's doing it, but he does it just the same. Three or four days go by, but he doesn't feel ready to return home yet, and so he stays on in the rented room. The days turn into weeks, the weeks turn into months. One day Wakefield walks down his old street and sees his house decked out in mourning. It's his own funeral, and his wife had become a lonely widow. Years go by. Every now and then he crosses paths with his wife in town, and once, in the middle of a large crowd, he actually brushes up against her. But she doesn't recognize him. More years pass, more than twenty years, and little by little Wakefield has become an old man. One rainy night in autumn, as he's taking a walk through the empty streets, he happens to pass by his old house and peeks through the window. There's a nice warm fire burning in the fireplace, and he thinks to himself: how pleasant it would be if I were in there right now, sitting in one of those cozy chairs by the hearth, instead of standing out here in the rain. And so, without giving it any more thought than that, he walks up the steps of the house and knocks on the door.

And then?

That's it. That's the end of the story. The last thing we see is the door opening and Wakefield going inside with a crafty smile on his face.

And we never know what he says to his wife?

No. That's the end. Not another word. But he moved in again, we know that much, and remained a loving spouse until death.

By now the sky has begun to darken overhead, and night is fast approaching. A last glimmer of pink remains in the west, but the day is as good as done. Black, taking his cue from the darkness, stands up from his spot and extends his hand to Blue.

It's been a pleasure talking to you, he says. I had no idea we'd been sitting here so long.

The pleasure's been mine, says Blue, relieved that the conversation is over, for he knows that it won't be long now before his beard begins to slip, what with the summer heat and his nerves making him perspire into the glue.

My name is Black, says Black, shaking Blue's hand.

Mine's Jimmy, says Blue. Jimmy Rose.

I'll remember this little talk of ours for a long time, Jimmy, says Black.

I will, too, says Blue. You've given me a lot to think about.

God bless you, Jimmy Rose, says Black.

And God bless you, sir, says Blue.

And then, with one last handshake, they walk off in opposite directions, each one accompanied by his own thoughts.

Later that night, when Blue returns to his room, he decides that he had best bury Jimmy Rose now, get rid of him for good. The old tramp has served his purpose, but beyond this point it would not be wise to go.

Blue is glad to have made this initial contact with Black,

but the encounter did not quite have its desired effect, and all in all he feels rather shaken by it. For even though the talk had nothing to do with the case, Blue cannot help feeling that Black was actually referring to it all along—talking in riddles, so to speak, as though trying to tell Blue something, but not daring to say it out loud. Yes, Black was more than friendly, his manner was altogether pleasant, but still Blue cannot get rid of the thought that the man was on to him from the start. If so, then Black is surely one of the conspirators—for why else would he have gone on talking to Blue as he did? Not from loneliness, certainly. Assuming that Black is for real, then loneliness cannot be an issue. Everything about his life to this point has been part of a determined plan to remain alone, and it would be absurd to read his willingness to talk as an effort to escape the throes of solitude. Not at this late date, not after more than a year of avoiding all human contact. If Black is finally resolved to break out of his hermetic routine, then why would he begin by talking to a broken down old man on a street corner? No, Black knew that he was talking to Blue. And if he knew that, then he knows who Blue is. No two ways about it, Blue says to himself: he knows everything.

When the time comes for him to write his next report, Blue is forced to confront this dilemma. White never said anything about making contact with Black. Blue was to watch him, no more, no less, and he wonders now if he has not in fact broken the rules of his assignment. If he includes the conversation in his report, then White might object. On the other hand, if he does not put it in, and if Black is indeed working with White, then White will know immediately that Blue is lying. Blue mulls this over for a long time, but for all that he gets no closer to finding a solution. He's stuck, one way or the other, and he knows it. In the end, he decides to leave it out, but only because he still puts some meager hope in the fact that he has guessed wrong and that White and Black are not in it together. But this last little stab at optimism soon comes to naught. Three days after sending in the sanitized report, his weekly check comes in the mail, and inside the envelope there is also a note that says, Why do you lie?, and then Blue has proof beyond any shadow of a doubt. And from that moment on, Blue lives with the knowledge that he is drowning.

The next night he follows Black into Manhattan on the subway, dressed in his normal clothes, no longer feeling he has to hide anything. Black gets off at Times Square and wanders around for a while in the bright lights, the noise, the crowds of people surging this way and that. Blue, watching him as though his life depended on it, is never more than three or four steps behind him. At nine o'clock, Black enters the lobby of the Algonquin Hotel, and Blue follows him in. There's quite a crowd milling about, and tables are scarce, so when Black sits down in a corner nook that just that moment has become free, it seems perfectly natural for Blue to approach and politely ask if he can join him. Black has no objection and gestures with an indifferent shrug of the shoulders for Blue to take the chair opposite. For several minutes they say nothing to each other, waiting for someone to take their orders, in the meantime watching the women walk by in their summer dresses, inhaling the different perfumes that flit behind them in the air, and Blue feels no rush to jump into things, content to bide his time and let the business take its course. When the waiter at last comes to ask their pleasure, Black orders a Black and White on the rocks, and Blue cannot help but take this as a secret message that the fun is about to begin, all the while marveling at Black's effrontery, his crassness, his vulgar obsession. For the sake of symmetry, Blue orders the same drink. As he does so, he looks Black in the eyes, but Black gives nothing away, looking back at Blue with utter blankness, dead eyes that seem to say there is nothing behind them and that no matter how hard Blue looks, he will never find a thing.

This gambit nevertheless breaks the ice, and they begin by discussing the merits of various brands of scotch. Plausibly enough, one thing leads to another, and as they sit there chatting about the inconveniences of the New York summer season, the decor of the hotel, the Algonquin Indians who lived in the city long ago when it was all woods and fields, Blue slowly evolves into the character he wants to play for the night, settling on a jovial blowhard by the name of Snow, a life insurance salesman from Kenosha,

Wisconsin. Play dumb, Blue tells himself, for he knows that it would make no sense to reveal who he is, even though he knows that Black knows. It's got to be hide and seek, he says, hide and seek to the end.

They finish their first drink and order another round, followed by yet another, and as the talk ambles from actuarial tables to the life expectancies of men in different professions, Black lets fall a remark that turns the conversation in another direction.

I suppose I wouldn't be very high up on your list, he says.

Oh? says Blue, having no idea what to expect. What kind of work do you do?

I'm a private detective, says Black, point blank, all cool and collected, and for a brief moment Blue is tempted to throw his drink in Black's face, he's that peeved, that burned at the man's gall.

You don't say! Blue exclaims, quickly recovering and managing to feign a bumpkin's surprise. A private detective. Imagine that. In the flesh. Just think of what the wife will say when I tell her. Me in New York having drinks with a private eye. She'll never believe it.

What I'm trying to say, says Black rather abruptly, is that I don't imagine my life expectancy is very great. At least not according to your statistics.

Probably not, Blue blusters on. But think of the excitement! There's more to life than living a long time, you know. Half the men in America would give ten years off their retirement to live the way you do. Cracking cases, living by your wits, seducing women, pumping bad guys full of lead—God, there's a lot to be said for it.

That's all make-believe, says Black. Real detective work can be pretty dull.

Well, every job has its routines, Blue continues. But in your case at least you know that all the hard work will eventually lead to something out of the ordinary.

Sometimes yes, sometimes no. But most of the time it's no. Take the case I'm working on now. I've been at it for more than a year already, and nothing could be more boring. I'm so bored that sometimes I think I'm losing my mind.

How so?

Well, figure it out for yourself. My job is to watch someone, no one in particular as far as I can tell, and send in a report about him every week. Just that. Watch this guy and write about it. Not one damned thing more.

What's so terrible about that?

He doesn't do anything, that's what. He just sits in his room all day and writes. It's enough to drive you crazy.

It could be that he's leading you along. You know, lulling you to sleep before springing into action.

That's what I thought at first. But now I'm sure that nothing's going to happen—not ever. I can feel it in my bones.

That's too bad, says Blue sympathetically. Maybe you should resign from the case.

I'm thinking about it. I'm also thinking that maybe I should just chuck the whole business and go into something else. Some other line of work. Sell insurance, maybe, or run off to join the circus.

I never realized it could get as bad as that, says Blue, shaking his head. But tell me, why aren't you watching your man now? Shouldn't you be keeping an eye on him?

That's just the point, answers Black. I don't even have to bother anymore. I've been watching him for so long now that I know him better than I know myself. All I have to do is think about him, and I know what he's doing, I know where he is, I know everything. It's come to the point that I can watch him with my eyes closed.

Do you know where he is now?

At home. The same as usual. Sitting in his room and writing.

What's he writing about?

I'm not sure, but I have a pretty good idea. I think he's writing about himself. The story of his life. That's the only possible answer. Nothing else would fit.

So why all the mystery?

I don't know, says Black, and for the first time his voice betrays some emotion, catching ever so slightly on the words.

It all boils down to one question, then, doesn't it? says Blue, forgetting all about Snow now and looking Black straight in the eyes. Does he know you're watching him or not?

Black turns away, unable to look at Blue anymore, and says with a suddenly trembling voice: Of course he knows. That's the whole point, isn't it? He's got to know, or else nothing makes sense.

Why?

Because he needs me, says Black, still looking away. He needs my eyes looking at him. He needs me to prove he's alive.

Blue sees a tear fall down Black's cheek, but before he can say anything, before he can begin to press home his advantage, Black stands up hastily and excuses himself, saying that he has to make a telephone call. Blue waits in his chair for ten or fifteen minutes, but he knows that he's wasting his time. Black won't be back. The conversation is over, and no matter how long he sits there, nothing more will happen tonight.

Blue pays for the drinks and then heads back to Brooklyn. As he turns down Orange Street, he looks up at Black's window and sees that everything is dark. No matter, says Blue, he'll return before long. We haven't come to the end yet. The party is only beginning. Wait until the champagne is opened, and then we'll see what's what.

Once inside, Blue paces back and forth, trying to plot his

next move. It seems to him that Black has finally made a mistake, but he is not quite certain. For in spite of the evidence, Blue cannot shrug the feeling that it was all done on purpose, and that Black has now begun to call out to him, leading him along, so to speak, urging him on towards whatever end he is planning.

Still, he has broken through to something, and for the first time since the case began he is no longer standing where he was. Ordinarily, Blue would be celebrating this little triumph of his, but it turns out that he is in no mood for patting himself on the back tonight. More than anything else, he feels sad, he feels drained of enthusiasm, he feels disappointed in the world. Somehow, the facts have finally let him down, and he finds it hard not to take it personally, knowing full well that however he might present the case to himself, he is a part of it, too. Then he walks to the window, looks out across the street, and sees that the lights are now on in Black's room.

He lies down on his bed and thinks: good-bye, Mr. White. You were never really there, were you? There never was such a man as White. And then: poor Black. Poor soul. Poor blighted no one. And then, as his eyes grow heavy and sleep begins to wash over him, he thinks how strange it is that everything has its own color. Everything we see, everything we touch—everything in the world has its own color. Struggling to stay awake a little longer, he begins to

make a list. Take blue for example, he says. There are
bluebirds and blue jays and blue herons. There are corn-
flowers and periwinkles. There is noon over New York.
There are blueberries, huckleberries, and the Pacific
Ocean. There are blue devils and blue ribbons and blue
bloods. There is a voice singing the blues. There is my
father's police uniform. There are blue laws and blue
movies. There are my eyes and my name. He pauses,
suddenly at a loss for more blue things, and then moves on
to white. There are seagulls, he says, and terns and storks
and cockatoos. There are the walls of this room and the
sheets on my bed. There are lilies-of-the-valley, carnations,
and the petals of daisies. There is the flag of peace and
Chinese death. There is mother's milk and semen. There
are my teeth. There are the whites of my eyes. There are
white bass and white pines and white ants. There is the
President's house and white rot. There are white lies and
white heat. Then, without hesitating, he moves on to black,
beginning with black books, the black market, and the
Black Hand. There is night over New York, he says. There
are the Chicago Black Sox. There are blackberries and
crows, blackouts and black marks, Black Tuesday and the
Black Death. There is blackmail. There is my hair. There
is the ink that comes out of a pen. There is the world a blind
man sees. Then, finally growing tired of the game, he begins
to drift, saying to himself that there is no end to it. He falls

asleep, dreams of things that happened long ago, and then, in the middle of the night, wakes up suddenly and begins pacing the room again, thinking about what he will do next.

Morning comes, and Blue starts busying himself with another disguise. This time it's the Fuller brush man, a trick he has used before, and for the next two hours he patiently goes about giving himself a bald head, a moustache, and age lines around his eyes and mouth, sitting in front of his little mirror like an old-time vaudevillian on tour. Shortly after eleven o'clock, he gathers up his case of brushes and walks across the street to Black's building. Picking the lock on the front door is child's play for Blue, no more than a matter of seconds, and as he slips into the hallway he can't help feeling something of the old thrill. No tough stuff, he reminds himself, as he starts climbing the stairs to Black's floor. This visit is only to get a look inside, to stake out the room for future reference. Still, there's an excitement to the moment that Blue can't quite suppress. For it's more than just seeing the room, he knows—it's the thought of being there himself, of standing inside those four walls, of breathing the same air as Black. From now on, he thinks, everything that happens will affect everything else. The door will open, and after that Black will be inside of him forever.

He knocks, the door opens, and suddenly there is no more distance, the thing and the thought of the thing are one and the same. Then it's Black who is there, standing in the doorway with an uncapped fountain pen in his right hand, as though interrupted in his work, and yet with a look in his eyes that tells Blue he's been expecting him, resigned to the hard truth, but no longer seeming to care.

Blue launches into his patter about the brushes, pointing to the case, offering apologies, asking admittance, all in the same breath, with that rapid saleman's pitch he's done a thousand times before. Black calmly lets him in, saying he might be interested in a toothbrush, and as Blue steps across the sill, he goes rattling on about hair brushes and clothes brushes, anything to keep the words flowing, for in that way he can leave the rest of himself free to take in the room, observe the observable, think, all the while diverting Black from his true purpose.

The room is much as he imagined it would be, though perhaps even more austere. Nothing on the walls, for example, which surprises him a little, since he always thought there would be a picture or two, an image of some kind just to break the monotony, a nature scene perhaps, or else a portrait of someone Black might once have loved. Blue was always curious to know what the picture would be, thinking it might be a valuable clue, but now that he sees there is nothing, he understands that this is what he should have expected all along. Other than that, there's precious little to contradict his former notions. It's the same monk's cell he saw in his mind: the small, neatly made bed in one corner, the kitchenette in another corner, everything spotless, not a crumb to be seen. Then, in the center of the room facing the window, the wooden table with a single stiff-backed wooden chair. Pencils, pens, a typewriter. A bureau, a night table, a lamp. A bookcase on the north wall, but no more than several books in it: Walden, Leaves of Grass, Twice-Told Tales, a few others. No telephone, no radio, no magazines. On the table, neatly stacked around the edges, piles of paper: some blank, some written on, some typed, some in longhand. Hundreds of pages, perhaps thousands. But you can't call this a life, thinks Blue. You can't really call it anything. It's a no man's land, the place you come to at the end of the world.

They look through the toothbrushes, and Black finally chooses a red one. From there they start examining the various clothes brushes, with Blue giving demonstrations on his own suit. For a man as neat as yourself, says Blue, I should think you'd find it indispensable. But Black says he's managed so far without one. On the other hand, maybe he'd like to consider a hair brush, and so they go through the possibilities in the sample case, discussing the different sizes and shapes, the different kinds of bristles, and so on. Blue is already done with his real business, of course, but he goes through the motions nevertheless, wanting to do the thing right, even if it doesn't matter. Still, after Black has paid for the brushes and Blue is packing up his case to go, he can't resist making one little remark. You seem to be a writer, he says, gesturing to the table, and Black says yes, that's right, he's a writer.

It looks like a big book, Blue continues.

Yes, says Black. I've been working on it for many years.

Are you almost finished?

I'm getting there, Black says thoughtfully. But sometimes it's hard to know where you are. I think I'm almost done, and then I realize I've left out something important, and so I have to go back to the beginning again. But yes, I do dream of finishing it one day. One day soon, perhaps.

I hope I get a chance to read it, says Blue.

Anything is possible, says Black. But first of all, I've got to finish it. There are days when I don't even know if I'll live that long.

Well, we never know, do we? says Blue, nodding philosophically. One day we're alive, and the next day we're dead. It happens to all of us.

Very true, says Black. It happens to all of us.

They're standing by the door now, and something in Blue wants to go on making inane remarks of this sort. Playing the buffoon is enjoyable, he realizes, but at the same time there's an urge to toy with Black, to prove that nothing has escaped him—for deep down Blue wants Black to know that he's just as smart as he is, that he can match wits with him every step of the way. But Blue manages to fight back the impulse and hold his tongue, nodding politely in thanks for the sales, and then makes his exit. That's the end of the Fuller brush man, and less than an hour later he is discarded into the same bag that holds the remains of Jimmy Rose. Blue knows that no more disguises will be needed. The next step is inevitable, and the only thing that matters now is to choose the right moment.

But three nights later, when he finally gets his chance, Blue realizes that he's scared. Black goes out at nine o'clock, walks down the street, and vanishes around the corner. Although Blue knows that this is a direct signal, that Black is practically begging him to make his move, he also feels that it could be a set-up, and now, at the last possible moment, when only just before he was filled with confidence, almost swaggering with a sense of his own power, he sinks into a fresh torment of self-doubt. Why should he suddenly begin to trust Black? What earthly cause could there be for him to think they are both working on the same side now? How has this happened, and why does he find himself so obsequiously at Black's bidding once again? Then, from out of the blue, he begins to consider another possibility. What if he just simply left? What if he stood up, went out the door, and walked away from the whole business? He ponders this thought for a while, testing it out in his mind, and little by little he begins to tremble, overcome by terror and happiness, like a slave stumbling onto a vision of his own freedom. He imagines himself somewhere else, far away from here, walking through the woods and swinging an axe over his shoulder. Alone and free, his own man at last. He would build his life from the bottom up, an exile, a pioneer, a pilgrim in the new world. But that is as far as he gets. For no sooner does he begin to walk through these woods in the middle of nowhere than he feels that Black is there, too, hiding behind some tree, stalking invisibly through some thicket, waiting for Blue to lie down and close his eyes before sneaking up on him and slitting his throat. It goes on and on, Blue thinks. If he doesn't take care of Black now, there will never be any end to it. This is what the ancients called fate, and every hero must submit to it. There is no choice, and if there is anything to be done, it is only the one thing that leaves no choice. But Blue is loathe to acknowledge it. He struggles against it, he rejects it, he grows sick at heart. But that is only because he already knows, and to fight it is already to have accepted it, to want to say no is already to have said yes. And so Blue gradually comes round, at last giving in to the necessity of the thing to be done. But that is not to say he does not feel afraid. From this moment on, there is only one word that speaks for Blue, and that word is fear.

He has wasted valuable time, and now he must rush forth onto the street, hoping feverishly it is not too late. Black will not be gone forever, and who knows if he is not lurking around the corner, just waiting for the moment to pounce? Blue races up the steps of Black's building, fumbles awkwardly as he picks the front door lock, continually glancing over his shoulder, and then goes up the stairs to Black's floor. The second lock gives him more trouble than the first, though theoretically it should be simpler, an easy job even for the rawest beginner. This clumsiness tells Blue that he's losing control, letting it all get the better of him; but even though he knows it, there's little he can do but ride it out and hope that his hands will stop shaking. But it goes from bad to worse, and the moment he sets foot in Black's room, he feels everything go dark inside him, as though the night were pressing through his pores, sitting on top of him with a tremendous weight, and at the same time his head seems to be growing, filling with air as though about to detach itself from his body and float away. He takes one more step into the room and then blacks out, collapsing to the floor like a dead man.

His watch stops with the fall, and when he comes to he doesn't know how long he's been out. Dimly at first, he regains consciousness with a sense of having been here before, perhaps long ago, and as he sees the curtains fluttering by the open window and the shadows moving strangely on the ceiling, he thinks that he is lying in bed at home, back when he was a little boy, unable to sleep during the hot summer nights, and he imagines that if he listens hard enough he will be able to hear the voices of his mother and father talking quietly in the next room. But this lasts only a moment. He begins to feel the ache in his head, to register the disturbing queasiness in his stomach, and then, finally seeing where he is, to relive the panic that gripped him the moment he entered the room. He scrambles shakily to his feet, stumbling once or twice in the process, and tells himself he can't stay here, he's got to be going, yes, and right away. He grabs hold of the doorknob, but then, remembering suddenly why he came here in the first place, snatches the flashlight from his pocket and turns it on, waving it fitfully around the room until the light falls by chance on a pile of papers stacked neatly at the edge of Black's desk. Without thinking twice, Blue gathers up the papers with his free hand, saying to himself it doesn't matter, this will be a start, and then makes his way to the door.

Back in his room across the street, Blue pours himself a glass of brandy, sits down on his bed, and tells himself to be calm. He drinks off the brandy sip by sip and then pours himself another glass. As his panic begins to subside, he is left with a feeling of shame. He's botched it, he tells himself, and that's the long and the short of it. For the first time in his life he has not been equal to the moment, and it comes as a shock to him—to see himself as a failure, to realize that at bottom he's a coward.

He picks up the papers he has stolen, hoping to distract himself from these thoughts. But this only compounds the problem, for once he begins to read them, he sees they are nothing more than his own reports. There they are, one after the other, the weekly accounts, all spelled out in black and white, meaning nothing, saying nothing, as far from the truth of the case as silence would have been. Blue groans when he sees them, sinking down deep within himself, and then, in the face of what he finds there, begins to laugh, at first faintly, but with growing force, louder and louder, until he is gasping for breath, almost choking on it, as though trying to obliterate himself once and for all. Taking the papers firmly in his hand, he flings them up to the ceiling and watches the pile break apart, scatter, and come fluttering to the ground, page by miserable page.

It is not certain that Blue ever really recovers from the events of this night. And even if he does, it must be noted that several days go by before he returns to a semblance of his former self. In that time he does not shave, he does not change his clothes, he does not even contemplate stirring from his room. When the day comes for him to write his next report, he does not bother. It's finished now, he says, kicking one of the old reports on the floor, and I'll be damned if I ever write one of those again.

For the most part, he either lies on his bed or paces back and forth in his room. He looks at the various pictures he has tacked onto the walls since starting the case, studying each one in its turn, thinking about it for as long as he can, and then passing on to the next. There is the coroner from Philadelphia, Gold, with the death mask of the little boy. There is a snow-covered mountain, and in the upper right hand corner of the photograph, an inset of the French skier, his face enclosed in a small box. There is the Brooklyn Bridge, and next to it the two Roeblings, father and son. There is Blue's father, dressed in his police uniform and receiving a medal from the mayor of New York, Jimmy Walker. Again there is Blue's father, this time in his street clothes, standing with his arm around Blue's mother in the early days of their marriage, the two of them smiling brightly into the camera. There is a picture of Brown with his arm around Blue, taken in front of their office on the day Blue was made a partner. Below it there is an action shot of Jackie Robinson sliding into second base. Next to that there is a portrait of Walt Whitman. And finally, directly to the poet's left, there is a movie still of Robert Mitchum from one of the fan magazines: gun in hand, looking as though the world is about to cave in on him. There is no picture of the ex-future Mrs. Blue, but each time Blue makes a tour of his little gallery, he pauses in front of a certain blank spot on the wall and pretends that she, too, is there.

For several days, Blue does not bother to look out the window. He has enclosed himself so thoroughly in his own thoughts that Black no longer seems to be there. The drama is Blue's alone, and if Black is in some sense the cause of it, it's as though he has already played his part, spoken his lines, and made his exit from the stage. For Blue at this point can no longer accept Black's existence, and therefore he denies it. Having penetrated Black's room and stood there alone, having been, so to speak, in the sanctum of Black's solitude, he cannot respond to the darkness of that moment except by replacing it with a solitude of his own. To enter Black, then, was the equivalent of entering himself, and once inside himself, he can no longer conceive of being anywhere else. But this is precisely where Black is, even though Blue does not know it.

One afternoon, therefore, as if by chance, Blue comes closer to the window than he has in many days, happens to pause in front of it, and then, as if for old time's sake, parts the curtains and looks outside. The first thing he sees is Black—not inside his room, but sitting on the stoop of his building across the street, looking up at Blue's window. Is he finished, then? Blue wonders. Does this mean it's over?

Blue retrieves his binoculars from the back of the room and returns to the window. Bringing them into focus on Black, he studies the man's face for several minutes, first one feature and then another, the eyes, the lips, the nose, and so on, taking the face apart and then putting it back together. He is moved by the depth of Black's sadness, the way the eyes looking up at him seem so devoid of hope, and in spite of himself, caught unawares by this image, Blue feels compassion rising up in him, a rush of pity for that forlorn figure across the street. He wishes it were not so, however, wishes he had the courage to load his gun, take aim at Black, and fire a bullet through his head. He'd never know what hit him, Blue thinks, he'd be in heaven before he touched the ground. But as soon as he has played out this little scene in his mind, he begins to recoil from it. No, he realizes, that's not what he wishes at all. If not that, then—what? Still struggling against the surge of tender feelings, saying to himself that he wants to be left alone, that all he wants is peace and quiet, it gradually dawns on him that he has in fact been standing there for several minutes wondering if there is not some way that he might help Black, if it would not be possible for him to offer his hand in friendship. That would certainly turn the tables, Blue thinks, that would certainly stand the whole business on its head. But why not? Why not do the unexpected? To knock on the door, to erase the whole story—it's no less absurd than anything else. For the fact of the matter is, all the fight has been taken out of Blue. He no longer has the stomach for it. And, to all appearances, neither does Black. Just look at him, Blue says to himself. He's the saddest creature in the world. And then, the moment he says these words, he understands that he's also talking about himself.

Long after Black leaves the steps, therefore, turning around and reentering the building, Blue goes on staring at the vacant spot. An hour or two before dusk, he finally turns from the window, sees the disorder he has allowed his room to fall into, and spends the next hour straightening things up—washing the dishes, making the bed, putting away his clothes, removing the old reports from the floor. Then he goes into the bathroom, takes a long shower, shaves, and puts on fresh clothes, selecting his best blue suit for the occasion. Everything is different for him now, suddenly and irrevocably different. There is no more dread, no more trembling. Nothing but a calm assurance, a sense of rightness in the thing he is about to do.

Shortly after nightfall, he adjusts his tie one last time before the mirror and then leaves the room, going outside, crossing the street, and entering Black's building. He knows that Black is there, since a small lamp is on in his room, and as he walks up the stairs he tries to imagine the expression that will come over Black's face when he tells him what he has in mind. He knocks twice on the door, very politely, and then hears Black's voice from within: The door's open. Come in.

It is difficult to say exactly what Blue was expecting to find—but in all events, it was not this, not the thing that confronts him the moment he steps into the room. Black is there, sitting on his bed, and he's wearing the mask again, the same one Blue saw on the man in the post office, and in his right hand he's holding a gun, a thirty-eight revolver, enough to blow a man apart at such close range, and he's pointing it directly at Blue. Blue stops in his tracks, says nothing. So much for burying the hatchet, he thinks. So much for turning the tables.

Sit down in the chair, Blue, says Black, gesturing with the gun to the wooden desk chair. Blue has no choice, and so he sits—now facing Black, but too far away to make a lunge at him, too awkwardly positioned to do anything about the gun.

I've been waiting for you, says Black. I'm glad you finally made it.

I figured as much, answers Blue.

Are you surprised?

Not really. At least not at you. Myself maybe—but only because I'm so stupid. You see, I came here tonight in friendship.

But of course you did, says Black, in a slightly mocking voice. Of course we're friends. We've been friends from the beginning, haven't we? The very best of friends.

If this is how you treat your friends, says Blue, then lucky for me I'm not one of your enemies.

Very funny.

That's right, I'm the original funny man. You can always count on a lot of laughs when I'm around.

And the mask—aren't you going to ask me about the mask?

I don't see why. If you want to wear that thing, it's not my problem.

But you have to look at it, don't you?

Why ask questions when you already know the answer?

It's grotesque, isn't it?

Of course it's grotesque.

And frightening to look at.

Yes, very frightening.

Good. I like you, Blue. I always knew you were the right one for me. A man after my own heart.

If you stopped waving that gun around, maybe I'd start feeling the same about you.

I'm sorry, I can't do that. It's too late now.

Which means?

I don't need you anymore, Blue.

It might not be so easy to get rid of me, you know. You got me into this, and now you're stuck with me.

No, Blue, you're wrong. Everything is over now.

Stop the doubletalk.

It's finished. The whole thing is played out. There's nothing more to be done.

Since when?

Since now. Since this moment.

You're out of your mind.

No, Blue. If anything, I'm in my mind, too much in my mind. It's used me up, and now there's nothing left. But you know that, Blue, you know that better than anyone.

So why don't you just pull the trigger?

When I'm ready, I will.

And then walk out of here leaving my body on the floor? Fat chance.

Oh no, Blue. You don't understand. It's going to be the two of us together, just like always.

But you're forgetting something, aren't you?

Forgetting what?

You're supposed to tell me the story. Isn't that how it's supposed to end? You tell me the story, and then we say good-bye.

You know it already, Blue. Don't you understand that? You know the story by heart.

Then why did you bother in the first place?

Don't ask stupid questions.

And me—what was I there for? Comic relief?

No, Blue, I've needed you from the beginning. If it hadn't been for you, I couldn't have done it.

Needed me for what?

To remind me of what I was supposed to be doing. Every time I looked up, you were there, watching me, following me, always in sight, boring into me with your eyes. You were the whole world to me, Blue, and I turned you into my death. You're the one thing that doesn't change, the one thing that turns everything inside out.

And now there's nothing left. You've written your suicide note, and that's the end of it.

Exactly.

You're a fool. You're a goddamned, miserable fool.

I know that. But no more than anyone else. Are you going to sit there and tell me that you're smarter than I am? At least I know what I've been doing. I've had my job to do, and I've done it. But you're nowhere, Blue. You've been lost from the first day.

Why don't you pull the trigger, then, you bastard? says

Blue, suddenly standing up and pounding his chest in anger, daring Black to kill him. Why don't you shoot me now and get it over with?

Blue then takes a step towards Black, and when the bullet doesn't come, he takes another, and then another, screaming at the masked man to shoot, no longer caring if he lives or dies. A moment later, he's right up against him. Without hesitating he swats the gun out of Black's hand, grabs him by the collar, and yanks him to his feet. Black tries to resist, tries to struggle against Blue, but Blue is too strong for him, all crazy with the passion of his anger, as though turned into someone else, and as the first blows begin to land on Black's face and groin and stomach, the man can do nothing, and not long after that he's out cold on the floor. But that does not prevent Blue from continuing the assault, battering the unconscious Black with his feet, picking him up and banging his head on the floor, pelting his body with one punch after another. Eventually, when Blue's fury begins to abate and he sees what he has done, he cannot say for certain whether Black is alive or dead. He removes the mask from Black's face and puts his ear against his mouth, listening for the sound of Black's breath. There seems to be something, but he can't tell if it's coming from Black or himself. If he's alive now, Blue thinks, it won't be for long. And if he's dead, then so be it.

Blue stands up, his suit all in tatters, and begins collecting the pages of Black's manuscript from the desk. This takes several minutes. When he has all of them, he turns off the lamp in the corner and leaves the room, not even bothering to give Black a last look.

It's past midnight when Blue gets back to his room across the street. He puts the manuscript down on the table, goes into the bathroom, and washes the blood off his hands. Then he changes his clothes, pours himself a glass of scotch, and sits down at the table with Black's book. Time is short. They'll be coming before he knows it, and then there will be hell to pay. Still, he does not let this interfere with the business at hand.

He reads the story right through, every word of it from beginning to end. By the time he finishes, dawn has come, and the room has begun to brighten. He hears a bird sing, he hears footsteps going down the street, he hears a car driving across the Brooklyn Bridge. Black was right, he says to himself. I knew it all by heart.

But the story is not yet over. There is still the final moment, and that will not come until Blue leaves the room. Such is the way of the world: not one moment more, not one moment less. When Blue stands up from his chair, puts on his hat, and walks through the door, that will be the end of it.

Where he goes after that is not important. For we must remember that all this took place more than thirty years ago, back in the days of our earliest childhood. Anything is possible, therefore. I myself prefer to think that he went far away, boarding a train that morning and going out West to start a new life. It is even possible that America was not the end of it. In my secret dreams, I like to think of Blue booking passage on some ship and sailing to China. Let it be China, then, and we'll leave it at that. For now is the moment that Blue stands up from his chair, puts on his hat, and walks through the door. And from this moment on, we know nothing.